A BAD BOY FOR CHRISTMAS

ALEX WOLF

ALEX WOLF

He's at the top of the naughty list.
Checks off all the boxes on the "you should run far away" checklist.
Best friend's new stepbrother.
Broody.
Hot as sin.
Mysterious past.
Pissed off at the world.
Everyone says he's trouble.
Parker even has the leather jacket for crying out loud.
I can't take my eyes off him, though. When he's in the room, I can feel his gaze on me at all times, heating me from within.
All I wanted to do was come home for the holidays and spend Christmas with friends and family, before I had to go out in the real world and put my degrees to use.
We're polar opposites. There's no way it would ever work between us.
But, the first time he touches me, and electricity blooms across my skin, I know one thing…
All I want for Christmas is him.

LAKE

Have you ever seen someone who stops you dead in your tracks? Makes your heart thump like a drum the second their eyes lock onto yours?

I have.

Once.

I drove through my hometown of Hope, Indiana. It had changed, and it hadn't. It was the week before Thanksgiving and they were already putting up decorations for the Christmas festival. That's the type of place Hope was. It didn't upset me at all. Christmas was my favorite time of the year, far superior to Thanksgiving in the holiday hierarchy.

I made my way through the older part of town and out to a new housing development. They'd built it while I was away at college. The place was growing fast and losing some of its small-town appeal, but at least it was holding on to traditions.

I rounded a corner to the street I was looking for and parked on the curb. I walked up the sidewalk in front of Cassie's house. A hint of fall still hung in the air, but I could almost smell the snow coming in the next month, followed by Christmas. I'd stopped for a few minutes at my parents' house, just enough to drop off a few suitcases. They weren't home, so I figured I'd head to Cassie's. I'd spent six years away from my best friend. I'd only seen her on occasional long weekends and school breaks. It was hell. We'd been inseparable since kindergarten.

Now, we'd be back to our old routine, hanging out every day, going on the post-grad job hunt. Her dad recently remarried and they'd moved to this subdivision. I glanced down the block. The houses were all cardboard cutouts of each other. Probably one builder with a common floorplan. Minor adjustments for each. They were all painted boring neutral colors, with new trees all the same height, one in each yard.

I raised a hand to knock and the door flew open so hard I nearly stumbled backward.

"Bitch!" Cassie grinned from ear-to-ear.

We basically tackled each other. Neither of us usually did the whole girly routine, complete with squealing and hopping up and down, but we did wrap each other up in an impressive bear hug.

"Come in." She waved me forward.

I stepped through the entryway and shrugged off my coat. The place was immaculate. New. It had that *new* smell to it. The subdivision had to be less than a year old. I could still see the lines from the sod as I'd walked up.

We both plopped down on the couch at the same time.

"Graduates." Cassie stared at me, beaming.

I returned her grin. "Yep." We'd both spent the summer getting our final credits, then I'd done a two-month internship I couldn't pass up.

"It's a bit anti-climactic, right?"

"Yep."

Cassie had returned home with a newly minted MBA. As for me, a master's degree in interior design. Years of work, student loans, and for what? Here we were. Homeless and jobless. The student loan bills would start up in six months.

"They always said the real work begins once you graduate."

I nodded. It was true. After graduating you felt like you'd won this huge battle, and money and respect and commendations were just waiting once you walked across that stage. Nope. It didn't work that way. It was like starting all over.

I glanced around the room. It wasn't very interesting. The usual leather furniture, pictures, a flat-screen TV on the wall.

Still, Cassie's smile, I'd missed it. I'd missed her. We talked on the phone every day and messaged on Facebook, but she had an energy about her that I hadn't been around in a while.

"So—" She waggled her eyebrows. "How's Danny?"

I looked away. "Yeah, about that."

"Really?" She tucked her knees up under her. "He have a small dick?"

My face had to have turned eight shades of pink. I shook my head. "I don't know."

"You didn't even get laid?"

I glanced to my fingers. The only action I'd had the past six months. They were loyal fingers, I had to give them that. They hadn't been inside any brunette coeds they were supposed to be 'studying' with. I shook my head at her again.

"It's okay. Luckily you have me to help get you back in the saddle."

I sighed. "I'm swearing off men for a while."

"My ass you are."

Right then, right at that moment, it hit me. I hadn't even seen him yet, but I felt it. Felt a presence. The temperature in the room shot up twenty degrees in a fraction of a second; hot enough to melt ice on a windshield. Clammy palms, cold sweat on the forehead, thighs tightening. The heat from his eyes seared into me and funneled straight down between my legs. I caught a glimpse of him peeking around the corner.

Holy hell.

Who is that?

My throat swelled shut. I gulped.

Two eyes.

Slate grey.

Dark hair slicked back.

His look said, *"Who the fuck is making all the noise?"*

My eyes flicked back over to Cassie. My face had to be white as a sheet. She stared around for a second, and then her gaze found him. "You can come say hi. This is Lake. My best friend since kindergarten."

I glanced back up to him and got hit with another round of the blowtorch gaze. "H-hi."

I couldn't look away. I couldn't do anything. My body was numb, frozen in time. I'd be damned if he wasn't the most beautiful man I'd ever seen. Some guys just have that look about them. A hundred percent male—primal. I knew Cassie had a new stepbrother, but she never said anything more than that. He looked mean and angry. So not my type. I'd never fallen for any type of bad boy, but he was like every cliché rolled up into one. He stepped out from the hall. Tight black V-neck stretched across broad shoulders. Levi's hugging his legs just right. Work boots.

Fucking hell, they looked worn in too. Like he *actually* worked for a living. Grease under his fingernails.

Cassie glanced up at him. "Fix the car?"

He didn't say anything. Just stared at me for a second. Then he grunted his disapproval and walked back into the hallway.

Come back.

I felt myself leaning toward the hallway, trying to will him back into the room. The temperature dropped back to regular levels and my blood began to circulate once more.

Cassie frowned at him, then looked over and caught me staring at his back. "Forget about it. He's bad news."

"Huh?" I realized I was still fixated on where he'd been. I snapped my head over to Cassie who had a shit-eating grin plastered across her face. "What?"

Her arms folded across her chest. It pushed her boobs up tight against some sorority letters. "He's my *brother*."

Shit.

What was I thinking anyway? There's no way. My parents would've thrown me out of the house if I'd brought a guy like that home.

"Where have you been keeping *him*?" The words came out before I could stop them.

Cassie leaned over. "I know. Okay, trust me. But just, no. He's trouble."

My mind was in a haze. "What's he even doing here? Who is he?"

She stared at me funny. "My brother. *Step* brother. He's not going to be here long."

"Why?" The word came out fast and almost territorial.

Pull yourself together.

"God, you're like a dog in heat. I've never seen you like this. He'll be gone shortly. We'll find you a, umm, better match. I promise."

I didn't want any other match. I'd always laughed about girls falling for the bad boy, or the rebel. It always seemed silly. We'd had new kids move to our town in high school. Mysterious guys. Guys who smoked. Guys who rode motorcycles. I'd never seen the appeal. I was more of the captain of the football team, or most likely to succeed type of girl anyway.

Practical.

That's what I'd always been. Practical Lake, who was on the honor roll, went to college, graduated, got a job, found a man who worked nine-to-five and treated me well, and off we sailed into the sunset. My life was on autopilot like that.

"What's his name?"

"Parker."

"How old is he?"

Cassie blew out a sigh. "We have to get you laid."

I woke up the next morning with a raging hard on. Fucking hell. I couldn't stop thinking about Lake. Which was pointless, because nothing could happen.

I was thirty years old and back to living with my mom and her new husband—and now, a stepsister. Temporarily, anyway. I stared at myself in the mirror. Where did the time go? I didn't even recognize myself. I was hardened. At one point in time I was a decent person, but now? Fuck that. Those days were long gone. People were nothing but shit.

I threw on some sweat pants and walked out into the living room.

"Going looking for a job today?" My mother's head turned, and I met her gaze.

"I have some things lined up. I'll be out of here soon. Don't worry."

"You know you can stay as long as you need to."

That's the thing about my mother. She'd say shit like that, but there was always context below the surface. She didn't want me there. She didn't want people to see her with me. I couldn't blame her. But, she'd still do her best to take care of me when I needed something.

I walked up and kissed her on the forehead. "I'm sorry."

She stared at me like she couldn't believe I was the man I'd become. It was fair. I needed to just disappear. Just get the fuck out of this place and let everyone else get on with their lives.

Lake.

Goddamn, that girl was gorgeous. The way her brunette hair fell in waves and flipped around when she stared at me. Her perfect tits, and high cheek bones. I'd always been a sucker for eyes, and hers were like an amber type of hazel. I couldn't get close enough, but I'd be willing to bet they had flecks of green in them.

The lips on that girl's mouth. Fuck.

I'd had a dream that she was staring up at me, lips parted, about to take my cock right into her mouth, and then I'd woken. I wasn't sure I'd ever cursed the morning sun that much in my life.

Hopefully, she wouldn't be around much. I didn't know if I could control myself around her. It'd been a long time since I'd had a woman in my bed, and making love wasn't my style. It'd never done anything for me. Wild, rough, and me doing whatever the fuck I wanted. That's what did it for me. I'd break her.

No, I most certainly would not be good for her. She looked like she was well put together, on her way to great things—success. She probably made straight A's and was on all that extracurricular bullshit. Probably had a list of things next to her name in the yearbook. Like president of this or that fucking club, and chairman of what the fuck ever. She was way out of my league, pretty much.

"What are you thinking about?"

"Huh?" I rolled my eyes back to Mom.

"I think you may have smiled for a second."

"Whatever." I walked off.

"Wait."

"Yeah?" I turned around.

"I need to talk to you for a minute." She bit one of her nails.

This should be great.

Biting a nail meant she was uncomfortable with the conversation we were about to have. She'd done it since I was a little kid.

"Yeah?"

"While you're living here—" She looked off at the ceiling, anything to avoid eye contact. "You need to be looking for a job."

"I have been. I told you I have a few things lined up."

"I know. There's one other thing—"

"What is it?"

"Paul, umm, he doesn't want you hanging out with Cassie." Her fingers trembled at her side.

Despite my hatred for the world, I didn't like to see my mom uneasy. I was sure Paul told her this was a condition of me moving in temporarily. It made sense. If I had a daughter, I wouldn't want her hanging around me either.

I sighed. "It's fine, Mom."

"I'm sorry."

I reached out and put a hand on her shoulder. "It's fine. I promise."

She nodded but didn't look convinced of my words.

———

I strode around the corner of a strip mall on Birch Street. What was it with small towns naming streets after trees? The sky was gray and looked like it might spit out a few flurries. Some city worker across the street was stringing Christmas lights from pole to pole down the street. Fuck, it wasn't even Thanksgiving yet. Just a reminder I'd have to stare at people pretending to be happy for the next month, while they secretly stressed about buying the right shit for everyone.

I glanced up at the building when I found the address I was looking for. The ad in the classifieds said the place was for rent, and it was cheap. I figured there'd be competition for the space at the price it was listed. I needed an office of some kind, and I had enough saved up for a deposit. The landlord was supposed to meet me there.

I spotted him opening up the door. He was a chubby guy, bald, maybe mid-forties.

"How's it going?" I strode over toward him.

He eyed me up and down, taking in as much information as possible. "Parker?"

"In the flesh." I attempted a smile, something I rarely did.

"Have money for deposits?"

"Yes, sir."

He turned the key and pushed the door open. "It's not much. Price is firm. Deposits and two months rent up front. Yearly lease."

"Sounds good." I followed him inside.

It was perfect. Perfect size. Perfect price. I had to have it. I was starting up another import/export business. Basically, I bought shit from overseas that I could sell at a higher price to clients in the U.S. It was how I made my living before all the shit went down. This time, I wouldn't have an asshole partner and the worst luck of all time to fuck it up, though.

"Your business all legal?"

"Yes, sir."

"There's a bathroom back there. Small office. What you see is what you get. Pay the rent on time, first day of every month, you'll never see me."

"Sounds good. I'll take it."

He raked his eyes up and down me once more. "I have a few other people to show it to this afternoon."

"When will you know something?"

Both his hands went to his hips. "Tomorrow." He nodded. "Yeah, should know by then."

"Well, I'm clean, run a legit business, and I won't have to change anything in here. Just need a place for clients to swing by once in a while, and a mailing address."

"I'll keep it in mind. Thanks."

"I appreciate that." I didn't want to sound too desperate. He might try to raise the price.

I stared over to where I'd put my desk. All I could think about was bending Lake over it and fucking her until her name fell from my lips. That girl was going to be trouble.

Dad came home from work before Mom. He strode into the kitchen while I was pouring a glass of water and shrugged his coat off.

"Hey, Lake."

"Hey, how was work?" I turned around to greet him.

He looked worn and weathered. He'd aged a lot in the past six years since I'd left for school. It made me wish I'd made it home more often than I did.

He loosened his tie around his collar and dropped a briefcase and his jacket on the table. "Your mom not home yet?"

"Nope."

Dad was a financial planner. He basically handled everyone's finances and invested money for them. It sounds like we should be rich or something, but he just worked for a company and earned a salary and some commissions. I always felt like he'd had dreams of doing something else with his life. He could play a piano beautifully. But, he'd met Mom, and they were married fast. She got pregnant. Playing a piano doesn't pay the bills, so here we were.

"So, what are the career plans?"

I took a sip. "Trying to figure that out. I don't know if I'm ready to open up my own business."

His eyes lit up for a split-second. "I can help with that stuff, you know? It's kind of what I do."

I smiled back at him. "Oh, I'll definitely utilize your skillset. They didn't teach us anything about that stuff at school." I cringed as soon as I said it, because I knew a lesson was coming—or a lecture. Maybe both.

Dad shook his head. "Damn shame. Schools should teach something useful. Most kids can't even get out of high school and balance a damn checkbook."

I watched Dad's lips moving as he went on and on about how they should teach more about compound interest and less about Shakespeare. All I could think about was Parker. God, his eyes. The way they seared into me and heated me from head to toe was like nothing I'd ever experienced before. Euphoria rushed through my veins like a warm hug any time I'd thought about him since.

How was a man that beautiful even possible? And how could he look so angry and menacing?

I'd tried to nonchalantly grill Cassie about him, to see what kind of extra information I could get, but she was evasive. Something was off. It was almost like she didn't know much about him at all.

It only made me want to know more even though deep down, I knew I should let it go. To get a job in interior design, I'd have to move into a city. Maybe even a bigger city where there were more jobs and competition. Nobody used interior designers around here, and I was aiming high. Corporate or high net-worth individuals who would give my name to other people, that's who I wanted to eventually design for.

"Know what I mean, Lake?"

I shook my head and tried to snap out of all my Parker and career fantasies. "Yep. You're absolutely right, Dad."

He snickered.

"What?"

"You didn't hear a damn word of any of that, did you?"

I smiled. "Not really, no. Sorry."

"It's okay. You had that glazed look in your eyes that your mother gets when I start talking about being practical."

"You need to live on the wild side, Dad. Jump out of a plane, or round your bank balance to the nearest dollar."

He pointed a sarcastic finger at me. "Don't you dare joke about that."

I hugged him. I'd missed him. Missed being home. It was good to be here.

"What are your plans tonight?" He leaned back from our hug.

"Probably hang out with Cassie. I missed her."

"Don't you guys talk on that Twitbook whatever? I didn't know it was possible for anyone to miss anyone these days. I used to sit by the phone for hours waiting on your mom to call. Now, everyone has a damn phone on them all day. Ruins all the suspense."

I shook my head and grinned. Twitbook; that was awesome. "It's not the same as being in the same room."

"Okay, well good. I want to take your mom to dinner. You're welcome to come along."

I put a hand on Dad's shoulder. "Don't worry. I won't mess up your game. Take your woman out and show her a good time."

I felt a little bad about it. I should eat dinner with them. I'd just returned home. And I had an alternative agenda, somewhere in my subconscious. Sure, I wanted to hang out with Cassie. I really did. But maybe Parker would be there too.

———

I walked up to Cassie's porch in my Levi's, tight, red stretch tee, and a cute leather jacket. Despite its simplicity, the outfit I had on took far more time to pick out than any outfit I'd chosen in the last three years. At one point I had on a black mini dress, then looked in the mirror and shook my head at myself. It was way too cold for that.

For crying out loud, what was this guy doing to me? Cassie would've stabbed me and buried me in the back yard if I'd shown up in that dress. I wanted to look hot, but normal. Cassie was a hawk. She'd pick up on any little thing.

I knocked on the door.

Please be Parker.

I needed his eyes to burn into me one more time. I wanted to know what he smelled like, he hadn't come close enough last time.

It was Cassie.

I must've frowned without knowing it.

"Good to see you too, bitch."

I shook my head and grinned. "Sorry I'm late."

"You're fifteen minutes early."

"Right. Right. Sorry." I stepped inside the door.

I hate you for making me like this, Parker. Do not ask about him.

"What do you want to do tonight? Dad's making dinner. You can eat with us if you want."

"That sounds good to me."

"We can go out after? Get some drinks? Find you a man." She waggled her eyebrows.

No sign of Parker in the house. What the hell? "Yeah, sure." I wasn't really sure what I'd just agreed to. My eyes roamed the house for any sign of modern day James Dean and his brooding stare.

"He's not here right now."

All the air left my lungs and I sulked. Realizing this, I quickly tried to snap back to my normal posture. "What? Who?"

"You know who the hell I'm talking about." Cassie grabbed me by the shoulders. Shook me a little. "He. Is. Bad. News." She sighed. "It's not gonna happen."

"I don't know what you're talking about."

"Come sit down."

We walked into the living room and I sat down on the couch. Cassie plopped down next to me.

"I'm going to tell you everything I know, so you can get this shit out of your system and we can move on. I know Parker is gorgeous. You don't think I notice things? Yeah, he's hot as fucking shit and he's my step brother. Yeah, I said that. But my dad warned me. He's not even supposed to talk to me, let alone my friends. They're just helping him out for a little while until he moves on."

"Why? He seemed nice."

"Are you shitting me right now? He didn't even say hi the one time you met him. He grunted and walked off."

"It seemed like a nice grunt." I shrugged. Yeah, he'd been cold and acted like an asshole. But why? There had to be a reason he hated the world that much.

"You know, for someone as smart and put together as you are, you can be pretty clueless. I wish I could take a picture of the way you're being and use it against you for the rest of your life."

I gave in. "I know, okay? I know. But tell me you aren't curious about him."

"Of course, I am. But I don't want you to get hurt, and my dad acts like—I don't know, like he's dangerous or something. He's been away for a while. Dad wouldn't even tell me what it was."

"Okay, fine, I'll stay away from him."

She nodded. "Okay."

I leaned over. "You think he's in the mafia?"

"I'm going to kick the shit out of you."

We both doubled over in laughter.

———

Cassie and I flipped through her yearbook in her bedroom, reliving memories and telling all kinds of stories you don't talk about on a phone, but once you're back in the bedroom you grew up in, they just pour out of you.

Just as we'd relived the one party I snuck out to go to, that I couldn't even enjoy because I was so nervous we'd be caught, Cassie's dad opened the door.

"Dinner in fifteen."

"All right," Cassie said.

Her dad stood there for a quick second and let out a sigh. "Parker is eating with us." He looked down at Cassie, seemingly having a conversation with just his stare.

"Okay."

He shut the door.

Cassie glanced over at me.

"Well, he didn't seem too happy about our dinner guest."

Her eyebrows rose. "Just try not to ogle him through dinner. You'll give Dad a heart attack."

"I won't," I lied.

PARKER

I knew Paul was just protecting his daughter, but fuck, the guy was a prick.

Just keep your head down and endure this for a few days.

They had to invite *her* though.

Lake.

My cock stirred in my jeans every time she moved, every time she breathed. I couldn't stop staring at her neck, and down the small vee of her shirt that cut to her tits. High, firm tits. I wondered what they'd feel like in my mouth while she arched her back into me. What she'd sound like when I fucked her so hard she couldn't breathe.

Just a few more days. That's all I needed to endure. A few more days and I'd never see any of these people again, including Lake. Something about that stabbed into my gut like a sharp knife.

"Can you pass the potatoes, please?" Lake stared at me with those hazel eyes of hers.

When I looked up, she glanced away. Wouldn't look at me. I wondered what they'd told her. Cassie seemed like the type that liked to gossip. If she knew, Lake probably knew. I passed the fucking potatoes. More like I shoved them at her. She jumped a little when the bowl rattled around on the table.

Everyone glared like I was beneath them.

"How's everything going with your business?" Mom's eyes rolled over to me.

"Fine."

"Anything new?" She was trying.

Paul snorted his disgust at the topic at hand. Strange, considering I figured he probably couldn't wait to be rid of me.

Lake would look over at me every so often and her eyes would shoot away when I'd catch her. She'd barely said a word through all of dinner.

"Should be gone in a few days."

"You can stay as long as you need to."

Fuck, it was so embarrassing. I could practically feel the pity coming through Lake and Cassie's eyes. Thirty years old and I was living in a shit hole. A couple thousand bucks to my name and it was all earmarked for my business. My life wasn't supposed to be this way.

Paul glared, and then his lips curled up into some kind of grin. "Probably better than the food that you're used to. Nice, home-cooked meal, right?"

Fucking prick. Hold it together for Mom.

"It's good. Thanks." I kept my head down and shoveled the chicken and potatoes in as fast as possible.

"Lake and I are going to go out later." Cassie perked up across the table.

"Oh, that sounds fun. You two have a lot to catch up on." Mom beamed at the two of them.

"We have to find Lake a man. She keeps dating assholes."

Paul choked on his water at Cassie's words.

My eyes whipped up to Lake before I could stop myself. I gripped the fork so hard my knuckles turned white.

Like fuck she's going to find a new man. Whoa, what the hell is wrong with me? Like I can control who she dates.

But the thought of any man touching her, even breathing near her, sent rage coursing through my blood.

"Cassie. Language." Paul shook his head.

Cassie went on without missing a beat, talking about how they were going to go out drinking, catch up on things, check out guys. I stood up from the table.

"Thanks for the food."

I walked over to the sink and rinsed my dishes. Tried not to bang them around in the sink, but I wanted to break everything in front of me. I could feel Lake staring at my back. Finally, I just shoved the shit in the dishwasher and stormed off to the room they'd given me. How the fuck was I going to sleep knowing Lake was out talking to guys and drinking? I needed an apartment, fast, away from humanity.

———

I'd sat in my room reading for the past hour. I couldn't focus on anything the entire time. Lake was in the house. Only a few boards and some drywall separated me from the girl of my dreams. But that was just it, it was a dream. Nothing more.

Maybe when I was younger, before all the bullshit. Maybe I would've been good for her. But not now. Not ever. I read the same page over and over and nothing registered. I walked out to the living room. Paul and my mom had gone off to the casino or something. They both liked to gamble, and then look at me like I was the irresponsible one.

I tried not to eavesdrop on Cassie and Lake, but it was impossible. Cassie's voice was known to carry through walls. She was definitely a talker, and it was all unfiltered. I found it annoying, but only because of the whole situation—circumstances. She was pretty funny sometimes, in small doses.

"You look hot as fuck."

My ears perked up from the couch. The words seared into me, because all I could think about were all the men who'd be staring at her looking 'hot as fuck' all night. Lake murmured something I couldn't make out. She was very shy and reserved.

"Oh, shut up, bitch. Every guy in the place is going to want to fuck you."

My jaw ground so hard I thought I might shatter my teeth. I couldn't handle this shit. Maybe it was just because I hadn't been with a woman in so long.. I just needed to go out and fuck someone to get it out of my system. Maybe that'd be an option. I'd never had to try very hard with women. The problem was finding one I could trust. A good match. Someone I wanted to spend more than one night with.

Just as I was about to get up and go off on a pussy quest, Cassie and Lake walked out of her bedroom. Time froze. I couldn't have moved if I'd wanted. Lake's eyes met mine. My face had to be pale as a ghost.

My God, she was fucking beautiful, like a goddess. She had on a mini skirt cut halfway up her thigh, and a tight green top that covered one shoulder and left the other bare. It wrapped around one side of her neck and turned into some kind of weave pattern with the fabric on the back. Her eyes were now smoky with a hint of green that drew out her irises even more. Her hair was curled and bouncing down her back.

I glanced down to see black stiletto heels. My brain didn't seem able to imagine anything but me between her legs while those heels dug into my hips.

She could have breathed across my dick right then and I'd have exploded.

Cassie was dressed in something similar. They both giggled and laughed like it was a normal night of the week and started toward the closet door for their coats.

They were going to freeze in those outfits.

"Where you going?"

It wasn't a polite question. Not making casual conversation. It was a demand.

Cassie stopped in her tracks. Lake's breath hitched.

Fuck. I hadn't meant to be that mean about it, but I didn't feel bad about it either.

"Wherever we want." Cassie glared.

I shook my head, clearly not thinking about what I was doing. It just happened. "Not dressed like that."

My brain wasn't in control of my mouth anymore. My gaze seared into Lake the whole time. I was only talking about her. Cassie could do whatever the fuck she wanted for all I cared.

Cassie blurted out a half laugh, half scoff. Her eyes widened at me a little, and then she turned to Lake. "Come on."

I walked over to the closet and grabbed my jacket.

"Where are *you* going?" Cassie asked.

"With you."

"Like hell you are."

"Maybe this is a bad idea. I should just go home." Lake glanced back and forth between us, but she chewed on her lip when she looked at me.

"Bullshit. He's not telling us what to do, and he's not invited."

I walked up and stared down at Cassie. "I go. Or you don't go."

"Fuck you."

"I'll sit at another table. But two girls at a club isn't safe, especially when you're drinking."

Cassie looked like she might throw a punch.

Lake grabbed her by the forearm. "Hey, it's fine. Let him come."

Cassie's stare kept darting back and forth between us. Finally, she blew a wayward lock of hair out of her face. "Fine. But keep your distance."

The corners of Lake's mouth curled up ever so slightly.

She wants me too. But I can't do shit about it.

I needed to push her away before it became too much. That's how I'd do it. Be an asshole, and maybe she'd stay away until I was gone. But no way was she going out to a club dressed like that while I knew about it—without me there to watch out for her. I wouldn't try anything with Lake, but I could still prevent her from making a mistake. I could still look after her.

LAKE

I should've been pissed.

Parker was acting like he pretty much owned us. Like he was a parent or something. I didn't even know the damn guy. And yet, something about him, it just drew me in. It was like I was in a trance around him. Maybe because he was older—more mature. It was something.

I'd never had a man make me feel this way before. I wanted to shake him and demand his secrets. What made him this way? Why was he back at home? What was this big secret that not even Cassie knew about? Why was he considered dangerous?

Cassie drove, and I sat in the passenger seat. Parker was in the back. I could feel his eyes on the back of my neck the whole time. The heat funneled straight between my legs. All night long at dinner, he stared broodingly at his plate. When he'd catch me looking at him, my heart would flutter, and butterflies would go crazy in my belly.

Cassie turned into the parking lot, and I had to sort of agree with Parker a little bit. It wasn't my type of place at all; an abandoned warehouse turned into a club. The bass was already thumping in my chest and we were a good twenty feet away from the building. I preferred a more laid back, pub-type atmosphere.

"There'll be some guys in here tonight." Cassie waggled her eyebrows at me.

Parker let out a sigh in the backseat.

I caught a glimpse of him in the mirror and his eyes were up toward the ceiling, like he was trying to look away from us. A vein bulged on his neck and I could see his heart pounding away in it.

We got out of the car and I nearly fell over when I went to open the door and it shot away. Parker caught me with his free hand.

"What the hell?" I found my balance.

"Are you okay?" Parker was lightning fast and already on a knee on the ground in front of me. His fingers pressed into my hip and for a brief second, squeezed, and I could feel what it would be like if he grabbed me from behind.

My fingers trembled on the door. I could barely get out a word. My eyes rolled up to meet his. He stared at me with a look of genuine concern.

"I-I'm okay."

"C'mon!" Cassie tapped her foot with hands on each of her hips.

I righted myself and Parker stood up. He made a point of walking in front of us and subtly tried to shield us from the view of any bystanders.

I gripped both of my elbows and hurried with Cassie to the door. It got really cold once the sun had gone down, and my legs were freezing in the skirt.

A huge guy in a security shirt checked IDs at the door.

Parker handed his over first and the guy eyed it longer than anyone else's. It looked different from what I could see, and the man looked it over for five seconds and stared at Parker, before letting him pass. It wasn't a normal driver's license. I hadn't seen anything like it before.

When we got through, I said, "What was that all about?"

"I have an ID card, not a driver's license."

Weird, but whatever. We walked over and shrugged our jackets off and handed them to a lady checking coats.

"You stay at a different table. Don't be ruining our game." Cassie glared at Parker.

"Wouldn't think of it, princess." He scoffed.

Cassie rolled her eyes. "Whatever." She grabbed me by the hand and practically yanked me across the room toward the bar. There were standing pub tables everywhere, and track lighting and a giant dance floor in the middle. Scantily clad women were gyrating to some dub step beat.

It was so not my scene. But I wanted to make Cassie happy. We neared the bar and Parker cut us off. "Find somewhere to sit. I'll get the drinks." His look said *don't argue with me.*

"Whatever." Cassie rolled her eyes again. If she wasn't careful, they were going to get stuck that way.

"I can pay for my own." I stared at the ground when I said the words. I didn't want Parker pissed off at me, but I always paid my own way.

"I'm going to make sure nobody puts anything in them." He glared at both of us like a parent would scold a child.

"We're twenty-four." Cassie folded her arms over her chest. "And we both have fathers."

"Just go find a seat."

"Ugh." Cassie stormed off, dragging me along with her.

I stared at Parker from the table. A couple women my age ogled him from the corner of the bar. I wanted to claw their eyes out.

"You need to get your shit together. He's an asshole."

"I think it's kind of sweet that he wants to make sure we're safe." Who was I? It was so nothing I would usually say.

"You want his cock inside you."

I smacked her on the arm. "Cass!"

The first smile I'd gotten out of her all night.

"Seriously, it can't happen. You need to forget about it."

We had to yell to hear over the music. Her words faded into it. All I could do was watch Parker at the bar.

The women continued to gawk and one of them walked over to him. My nails dug into the wood on the table.

Cassie glanced down at my hand then back up at me. "You need to get laid so bad. But not him. Promise me, not him. Please."

"You know I would never do anything with your brother." It was the first promise I didn't know if I'd be able to keep with her. I had to, I knew that. But if I was in a room alone with him, I just didn't know. He pulled me out of my body when I stared at him. Turned me into a completely different person. An irrational person. I'd never experienced anything like his presence.

Our conversation was interrupted when a man walked up. He was gorgeous in his own right, but kind of a douche at the same time. Could spot the type from a mile away. Entitled, self-righteous. I hated judging people without talking to them, but in this kind of atmosphere, you had to be on your guard at all times.

Please talk to Cassie.

He was definitely her type. Looked wealthy. Slicked back, brown hair, blue eyes.

He leaned down to Cass's ear. "Wanna dance?"

"Hell yes!" Then her eyes flicked over to me and back to the bar. "Behave."

That's all she said to me. She did the thing where she pointed at both of her eyes and then back at me with the same two fingers as she walked toward the dance floor, like she'd be watching me.

Parker stalked back over to the table. He looked like he might actually smile when he noticed Cassie was gone. He carried two tumbler glasses that were pink. Fucking fruity drinks. What was it with men thinking all women drank mixed drinks? I preferred whiskey or beer. Anyway, I'd be surprised if they had alcohol in them at all.

My breaths sped up with each step he took. I needed a game plan. Yes! A plan. I was good at plans. Maybe my normal self was returning the more I was around him. It was just a quick bit of excitement, and then everything would revert back inside me, once all the chemicals firing in my body restored themselves to normal levels.

I had to keep my distance. I'd promised Cass. He was off limits. *Off limits!*

He set the drinks down harder than he needed to, and slid one over toward me. The pink liquid sloshed around in the glass and some of it spilled over the side. Parker didn't seem to notice.

"You're welcome."

I glared. *Tried* to glare anyway. God, he was so intense. So damn manly and broody.

"I didn't thank you."

He smirked. It lit me on fire inside, and not in a bad way. The two women were still ogling him from across the bar.

"What'd she say to you?" I glared at the woman that talked to my Parker.

My Parker?

I was so fucked. I needed to be rude to him. Let him know there was no way I was a possibility in his world.

He put a hand to his ear, gesturing that he couldn't hear what I'd asked. No way was I sliding over closer to him. I could feel Cass's eyes burning me from the dance floor while she dry-humped Preppy Boy's leg.

I turned back, and Parker was next to me, leaning down close.

Holy shit.

His head was next to my ear. He could lick my neck from there if he wanted. I was wet already, and he hadn't even said anything. If he spoke I'd feel his warm breath on me. Neurons fired through my limbs, and my muscles tensed.

"What'd you ask?"

The tiny hairs on my neck stood at attention, and goose-bumps pebbled down my arms. I gulped.

"What'd that girl say to you?" I had to yell even though he was sitting next to me.

"She wanted to buy me a drink."

I rolled my eyes. *Desperate.*

God, who am I? She could've been nice for all I knew.

"Don't worry, I told her no."

"I don't care if she buys you a drink. Pfft."

He leaned in closer and I thought I might combust. His lips were centimeters from my ear.

"Yeah you do."

My eyelashes fluttered at his breath, and I tried to stay calm. Maintain composure. My pussy throbbed merely at his presence. His stare sent heat straight to my clit. I couldn't even imagine if he actually touched me with those strong hands that gripped me in the parking lot. Digging into my hips.

I'd never had any inclination to be spanked. I'd always found it kind of silly. But fuck, if I didn't want Parker to do it. I wanted him to do everything to me. I'd never had a man just own me in the bedroom. It was always some responsible guy with a good resume spasming on top of me for a few minutes. It was okay, but it wasn't the type of sex you hear about. Mind-blowing, orgasmic sex, where you end up in a tangled mess of limbs, flushed with pink in the face at what you just did and may or may not have said during it.

I wanted to experience that, at least once. Who wouldn't?

"Why are you so angry?" I blurted out the words before I could stop myself.

Parker stared at me. Pierced me with his gaze, for the longest seconds of my life. He shook his head. "You wouldn't understand."

He started to walk away, but I grabbed his wrist. *What are you doing?*

My fingers lit up with flames when our skin touched. They flickered and licked hotter and higher, the snaking heat coursing through my body and blooming across my skin. Shocks of tingles radiating through my limbs just at touching him.

"I'm pretty smart. Try me."

His eyes narrowed. The collar of his shirt tightened on his neck. His forearm turned to steel in my hand, his whole body tensing. So much power in his body. So much energy begging to burst out of his skin.

"I'm no good for you." He sighed, stared at the ceiling then back at me. "No good for anyone."

I couldn't imagine what he must've done or gone through to feel that way. His mom seemed nice, surely they had some kind of bond.

"Wh-what's your—"

"What's what?" His words came through gritted teeth.

I should've stopped myself. Should've just said never mind. "What's your secret? The one that's bothering everyone?"

He looked away, stared around the room. Wouldn't look at me. It wasn't anger on his face. It was shame.

"Don't."

He was still looking away and my grip tightened on him. I didn't want him to look away. I wanted his eyes on me, always. When he looked away, the heat left my body. Summer turned to winter inside of me.

"Sorry, just making conversation." I let go of his arm.

His eyes moved to my hand, slowly and deliberately. Parker looked like he wanted to break something. He was so angry. But why?

He took a deep breath and turned back to me. "Tell me about you."

I glanced down. "Not much to tell, really." God, I wished we were at a bar where we didn't have to scream to hear one another. Lights danced around the walls, and it sounded like the song was about to end. I didn't want it to. Cassie would be back. This was the most I'd been able to talk to Parker.

"You just got back from college?"

"Yeah, grad school."

I wanted to know more about Parker, but he seemed relaxed when we talked about me. Like his guard was lowering. It sent a wave of joy through me that I could make him relax and stop staring at everything like he wanted to burn the world to ashes.

"What will you do now?"

"Look for a job."

"I'm sure you'll be great at whatever you do."

"Thank you." I knew it was just something everyone says when you graduate. But a compliment from Parker meant more for some strange, idiotic reason. Evil hormones and chemicals were still at work. I knew the biology behind it and didn't care. When he was around, I wanted his attention on me, and when it wasn't, I wanted him right back like someone had stolen my oxygen.

It was completely stupid, the more I thought about it. I'd known him for all of a day. It wasn't love. It was lust. But there was still something, something in the way our eyes first locked, that seemed like a spark. Something outside the realm of all the hormones and chemicals firing. Like I could see him. See who *he* was.

"And what is that?"

"Huh?"

"What is it you'll do?"

"Oh." I was so stupid. Of course, that would be the next question. "Interior design."

"That always been your dream?"

"Pretty much. I've always been good at that kind of thing. I can walk into a room and see the way it should be. The way I would make it, anyway." I stared at him for a second. He looked like he watched, heard, and processed every single word. It wasn't small talk. He was actually hearing me, however vague I was being. Like he wanted to know.

"What about you? What's your dream?"

His face tightened again, and I wanted to take back my question immediately. He seemed to get so upset when I pressed him for information about himself.

"Not important."

I shook my head. "Everyone is important."

I stirred the pink fufu drink with my straw. He leaned in to say something else and Cassie strode up. Her and her new dance partner were already coated in a fine sheen of sweat. The pretty boy hung back for a second, and Cass glared when she walked up.

"You're supposed to be at another table." She had to get right up next to us, before she said it, so we would hear.

"It's okay, really." I put a hand on her arm.

"Yeah, I bet it is." She half-scolded, half-smiled at me. Then she glared at Parker.

He started to walk off, and I wanted to grab him and yank him to the seat next to me.

"Come on. Preston has a friend. He wants to introduce you."

Parker froze in place. That vein on his neck bulged again, and now they snaked through his forearms as well. Thick forearms of nothing but corded muscle and knots and ridges.

My stomach screwed itself up nice and tight at his reaction, and at the fact I didn't want to go with Cass. I wanted to stay right there and talk to Parker. I never wanted to stop talking to him. "I'm fine right here." I looked at Parker while I said it. "I'm not really—"

Parker turned and stared at me. "Go."

My eyes widened. What the hell? I didn't know if he realized the game I was trying to run on Cassie at the moment. *No, Parker, I want to tell her no, so I can stay here with you.*

"Really, I just don't feel like dancing right now."

Parker looked away from us. Like he wouldn't be able to say it again if he could see me. "Go, have fun. I'll be right here."

Cass stared and tapped her foot. I looked back and forth between them, and then Cass held out her hand. I took it.

———

Parker wouldn't even look at me the whole time I danced. I tried to keep my distance from the guy. He seemed okay, but I didn't want to be there with him. He wore a long-sleeve button-down, rolled up his forearms, and gray slacks. Looked like he'd came to the club straight from work.

Cassie was grinding all over her partner. I tried to look for Parker, but the crowd had grown so thick, and the place was so dark, I couldn't see him any longer.

The guy I was with kept trying to move in closer and I'd back away. He had a drink in his hand. It smelled like whiskey and singed my nostrils any time I got close to it. Usually, I'd have loved the smell of whiskey, but the longer I was out there with him, the more the smell turned in my stomach as it mixed with the nerves. I wasn't sure why, but I felt like I was doing something wrong, like I was supposed to be with Parker, and instead I was on the dance floor with another man.

It was stupid. Totally irrational, and yet, I couldn't help how I felt.

What are his secrets?

I finally learned that this guy's name was Adam. He yelled it in my ear when he moved in close. I backed away once more, but somehow his full drink had vanished while my mind wandered elsewhere. He yanked me into him this time and his hands were all over me.

I started toward the dance floor as soon as that motherfucker pulled her in close. I'd been watching them out the corner of my eye, even though I tried not to. But as soon as I took a step in that direction, she shoved him away and stormed off toward the restrooms. I glared at the asshole, but took a deep breath, and then stalked around the dance floor, headed for the back. I couldn't beat the shit out of the guy, no matter how bad I wanted to. Lake saw me shoving through the crowd and her face went from anger to shame.

Just as I caught up to her, she pushed the door open to the women's bathroom and disappeared inside.

Fuck that. She wasn't going to sit in there alone after that.

I barged in right behind her.

"Hey!" A lady shouted the word from behind me as I stormed through the door.

I glanced around to make sure nobody else was in there. It was the last thing I needed. I leaned down and looked under the stalls—nobody else. I flipped the lock on the door.

Lake's head whipped over in my direction and her face was flushed. She stared off at the wall behind me. Her breathing was labored.

"You okay?" I strode over to her. She was leaned up against the wall next to the sink.

"I'm fine. You can't be in here."

"Says who?"

"Says the sign on the door." Her eyes moved up to me and quickly snapped away to the corner of the room.

I got up close and put my hand on the wall next to her. Forced her to look me in the eye.

"Do I look like I care about rules?"

She squirmed a little against the wall. Not in a way that suggested she wanted me out of there. It was a nervous gesture.

I leaned down next to her ear. Fuck she smelled so goddamn good. It was her shampoo. She wasn't wearing perfume. I wanted to bury my nose in her hair. I took a deep breath. Tried to compose my thoughts. She was a master of sending my mind reeling in a million different directions. Given my circumstances, I couldn't afford to break any kinds of rules. But I didn't give a shit when I was around her.

"I just want to make sure you're okay." My words still came out as a growl. It's just how I talked now. A forced habit. I didn't know how to be soft or gentle—human.

"I-I'm okay."

I tilted her chin up with my index finger. Stared at those hazel eyes. They looked like they could see right through me. See everything I was. I had to look away for just a second, just to get some reprieve.

"Did he hurt you?" My eyes shot to the door, looking for the dance floor beyond the walls.

"I can take care of myself."

I backed up a step, though it was incredibly difficult to do. "All right."

I turned to walk back out to the club. She was safe in the bathroom.

"I want to know more about you." Her words hit me in the back.

I couldn't turn around. Not then. I couldn't tell her about me. If she knew the truth, she wouldn't talk to me again, and I didn't want whatever this little connection was between us to ever end.

"You can't."

"Why?"

I still stared straight ahead with her at my back. "Not a good idea."

"I know you feel whatever this is between us. Don't lie and say you don't feel it too."

I sighed. Fuck yes, I felt it. I felt it in every bone in my body, it seeped into the marrow, it coursed through my blood, and pumped through my heart, every second since I saw her.

But I couldn't give in. It would never work.

"I don't know what you're talking about."

"Liar."

I closed my eyes. Her reaction stabbed me in the heart with a cold shard of glass. It twisted and twisted. *Don't turn around.*

"Just get out. Don't act like you care if you don't."

I heard a sniffle and turned my head back. A tear ran down her cheek. I marched over and wiped it from her face with my thumb before I could even think about my actions. "Don't cry. You should never have to hurt."

"Why are you lying? I see the way you look at me."

My hands balled into fists at my sides. I had to get the fuck out of this bathroom. "I'm no good for you, okay?" I pushed a stray strand of hair behind her ear even as I said the words I didn't want to say. "You should stay away from me."

I started to turn, and her hand reached for my wrist. A spark of electricity shot through my limbs just at her touch. It was too much. I couldn't bear to look at her upset for another moment.

"Why do you keep saying that?"

I tried to turn away. I had to get the fuck out of there. She didn't know how I was, what I would do.

"I have to go." I shook her hand off me.

"Why? Why are you being a fucking asshole right now?"

Blood rushed into my face. I spun around and slapped my hand on the wall next to her head. She jolted, and her eyes grew wide.

"I can't control myself around you." I raked my stare up and down her. "And I won't be gentle."

Her face flushed with pink hues and she wiped her palms down the side of her skirt.

"Maybe I don't want gentle."

I turned again.

You can't do this shit, man.

Her hand slapped on my forearm and her nails dug into me. "No. You're not walking away."

I whirled around and slammed my mouth onto hers. Microbursts of nerve firings ripped through my limbs just at the feeling of her lips on mine. My chest slammed her back against the wall. She let out a huge, breathy exhale coupled with a moan that caught in her throat.

I shoved my tongue against her mouth, demanding that she open for me, which she did. As fast as my mouth was on her lips, I moved to her neck and sucked and licked to her ear. Her hands searched my shoulders and back, nails full-on clawing into my shirt. Nothing but grasping and pulling anywhere she could find a hint of friction.

With one hand I fisted her hair, and the other went up her skirt straight to her ass. I dug my fingers into her soft flesh so hard it would definitely bruise tomorrow. Her back arched from the wall and her tits pressed against my chest.

"Is this what you want? Me to yank your hair and fuck you against this wall?"

"God, y-yes." Her words came out on a gasp.

My cock was so hard I thought my jeans might bust open at any second, with no effort on my part.

My hand slid down her ass. I could feel the heat radiating from her pussy before my fingers ever got there. I cupped her in my hand, like it was my possession, then shifted her panties to the side. Shoved two fingers into her as hard as I could and curled toward the ridge deep inside of her.

Fuck me, I'd never forget the way she felt, the way she looked, the way she gasped, the first time I had those two fingers inside her. I thought my cock might blow just at the feeling.

"Oh God, Parker."

I leaned into her ear with my fingers still buried to the hilt. "You wish this was my cock, don't you?"

She nodded, furiously.

I exhaled a breath down her neck, just to watch her skin pebble with anticipation.

I gripped her around the throat with my free hand. Not hard. Not forceful. Just enough to keep her head steady while I told her everything that'd be in store for her, if we ever had a chance to be alone.

"I'll tell you one time, why you have no business with me, Lake."

I gritted my teeth. My cock practically begged to shove inside of her.

"I'm not a nice man. I don't do easy, emotional, sex. I don't do feelings." I slid my hand from her throat to her hair and balled it into a fist. Pulled it back until her gaze was angled toward the ceiling and her throat was fully exposed. I licked from her collar bone to her ear. "I fuck hard. Ass, mouth, pussy, tits, anything I want. So goddamn rough you won't walk for a day. I pull hair, spank, bite, and choke. So don't tempt me again after this. Because it's not gonna happen with you."

She smacked me in the face. I slid my fingers out of her and backed away. Fuck, what had I just done? My stomach turned, and I rolled my eyes up to the ceiling. "I'm sorry, I shouldn't have—"

She shoved me but didn't run away. Her eyes were half-hooded, and her mouth slightly curled at the corners. "Fuck you, Parker. Maybe I want *that*."

Her stare was going to send me over the edge.

I backed away. I couldn't touch her again without doing all the things I'd just told her. "It's not going to fucking happen. So forget about it, Lake. Forget you ever fucking met me."

"Why? Is something wrong with me?"

I stood there, shaking my head. How could she not see it? She looked like she might cry again. I took a step toward her and put a hand on her shoulder. "No. There is nothing wrong with you. Nothing."

"So why then?"

"Because you deserve better than that. Better than this." I looked down at myself then back at her.

She started to respond, and a fist beat on the door. A man's voice rang out over the thumping of the bass.

"Hey, keep it moving in there. Let's go!"

Fuck me, I was sure we were going to get kicked out when I walked out with her. We had no choice, though. I grabbed Lake by the hand and pulled her toward the door.

Unlocked the deadbolt and walked out. Confidence was key. Act like you own the place. The security guy grabbed me by the arm. "No fucking in the bathrooms here. You guys are out."

"She lost a contact. I was helping her look."

"Bullshit. Heard that one a million times. You're no longer welcome here."

"Fuck." I was sure I'd hear about this from Cassie, and our parents if she told them.

Thankfully, Cassie saw us being marched out of the place and followed. They let us grab our coats, but not without the big bouncer standing there, glaring.

Cassie unloaded on me when we were shoved out the door. "Why'd you have to come? You ruined the night."

"Cassie, it wasn't his—"

"Bullshit. It was supposed to be our night. You're not our fucking dad. We're adults."

She had no idea what'd happened. Was too busy trying to get up on some yuppie fuckbag to even notice her friend was being groped. I couldn't stand there and listen to her shit anymore. "I'm going to get the car. Stay here in the light. Can you manage that, *Cassie?*"

"Fuck you! We can walk through a parking lot at night."

I got up in her face. Tried to be gentle, but gentle was something I would probably never be again, ever. "Don't move. I'll be right back."

Parker stomped off toward the car in the parking lot. I sat there, frozen. My mind still reeling from having his rough fingers shoved deep inside me. I was still wet and my clit pulsed under my skirt.

Jesus.

His words. His mouth. His tongue. I squirmed in the best possible way thinking about it. The way he'd stormed into the bathroom, and the way he now stalked toward the car; I was lost in him, and I wasn't sure I'd ever get out of this spell he had over me.

"Can you fucking believe him?"

I turned to Cassie. "Huh?"

"You need to stay away from him. I'm telling you."

About the time I was going to respond, two guys stumbled out of the bar.

"What do we have *here*?" The guy shouted the word 'here' and slurred his words.

They were wasted and reeked of booze. Something about them made me immediately feel uncomfortable and anxious.

God, please hurry, Parker.

The other guy smacked Cassie on the ass as they went by. She started to yell something at him, when the headlights hit us. Cassie got that look in her eyes. The look when she's about to do something stupid. She was definitely pissed off at Parker, and when Cassie was pissed, she let the other person know. It didn't happen often, but she had just enough alcohol in her bloodstream to do something stupid. It wasn't a good combination.

She spun the guy around and kissed him. His hands immediately went to her ass and cupped both cheeks in his palms.

It might not have been so bad when Parker pulled up, but the man's friend took it as a group invitation. He pulled me in for a kiss, and I shoved him away.

"Don't fight it. You know you want this."

I shoved at his chest, but he tightened his grip and grabbed my ass with his other hand.

The next few seconds were a blur. All I saw was a flash of black and heard, "Get the fuck off her!"

The guy hit the pavement.

His buddy held his hands up. "What the fuck, bro? They came onto us."

"Get in the fucking car," Parker growled at both of us.

"Don't tell us what to fucking do." Cassie glared at Parker.

I started for the car. Anything to get away from the two assholes. Groped twice in one night. I was never going to a club again. Cassie was on her own in that department. I knew she was trying to get back at Parker, but I didn't give a shit. They could figure out their dysfunctional family problems on their own time. I wanted no part of it.

I hopped in the car while Parker stared down the two guys. Cassie huffed and came in behind me. She slid up next to me in the backseat. Apparently, she didn't want to be in the front with Parker.

He glared at the two guys until he saw we were in the car, then headed for the driver's side.

"Can you fucking believe him?" Cassie turned to me.

"Whatever."

"Oh, you're taking his side?"

"I'm not taking any sides. I don't want any part of whatever you two have going on."

"It would've been fine if he hadn't brought his stupid ass along."

"I just got groped because you were trying to get back at him. I love you, Cass. But I don't appreciate that."

She sat there for a second, contemplating. Her face was still red with heat, but she let out a sigh. "Fuck, I'm sorry."

I looked away and shook my head. "It's fine."

"You know how I get when people try to make me do shit." She put a hand on my arm.

I glanced down at it then back up at her. Her apology was genuine, but I wasn't letting her off the hook that easy. "It's fine. Just keep me out of it next time."

"Okay. I'm sorry."

Parker's footsteps pounded the pavement so hard I swore I could feel them as he stomped to the car. This wouldn't be fun.

The whole car shook when he folded himself into the front seat and slammed the door. His hands gripped the steering wheel so hard I could see the whites of his knuckles. He stared around at the parking lot to see if anyone was watching, then reversed out and sped off onto a side street.

His eyes met mine in the rearview mirror and my body heated up once more. My legs squeezed together at the intensity in his gaze, and a rush of flames sizzled through my veins. I could feel his fingers inside me again, his words in my ear about all the things he would do to me. My pussy instinctively tightened around nothing but air. I thought I might melt into a puddle and slide down into the floorboard.

"How could both of you be so stupid?"

Oh shit.

"We were fine. You were the problem." Cassie's arms folded over her chest and she glared out the window.

Cassie was drunker than I thought. Her head started to bobble like all the drinks were catching up to her at once.

"Dressing like that and going to the club." Parker shook his head. "You're asking for trouble."

Cassie stiffened, her face turning bright red. "You're one to talk about trouble."

Parker's eyes widened, like maybe Cassie knew something she wasn't supposed to. There were barbs attached to her words and her voice was pure venom.

"Shut the fuck up. You don't know what you're talking about."

"Oh really?"

"Say another word and I'll throw your ass out of the car." Veins bulged up and down Parker's forearms and his neck.

I stared over at Cassie. Her jaw was flexed, like she was biting back everything she wanted to yell at him.

What did she know? What was she not telling me?

Cassie was always protective. Always tried to shield me from everything.

Seeing the way Parker reacted when she brought it up made me question even wanting to know. I thought it was pretty hot how he wanted to protect us—it was manly as hell. Parker was a magnet, drawing me closer to him by the minute. His eyes stayed fixed on me the whole time. So much I was wondering how he could drive at the same time.

The rest of the car ride was awkward silence. We got out of the car and went in first. I tried to hang back, but Parker stayed in the car with his head on the steering wheel. I didn't want him to feel bad. I wanted him to feel appreciated for what he did. At the same time, I didn't want to upset Cass. She was already stumbling into the house.

I helped her to bed.

Can't believe I lost my temper like that last night. For fuck's sake. Over a girl.

It was the last thing I could afford to have happen right then. What if I'd been arrested for throwing that guy to the pavement? I needed to keep my head on straight. Forget about Lake. Forget about everyone. I had a business to get up and running. I had to get out of my mom's house. Falling for a girl was going to jeopardize everything, especially one I'd just met.

But fuck, I'd never met anyone like her.

I waited in my bedroom until I heard Lake leave the next morning. She'd stayed the night to take care of Cassie. I had this fantasy in my head all night long, that she was going to slip into my room. It was no good, because we'd have to be quiet, and that was the exact opposite of what I wanted.

Once Lake left, I headed for a cold shower to tame the raging hard on that graced me all morning at the thought of Lake riding me. I had thirty minutes to get ready and go meet an old friend about business.

I showered in record time—basically, long enough for my dick to settle the fuck down—then threw on some clothes and headed out the door. The cold, watery sun socked me in the face the second I walked outside. How could it be so fucking bright and cold at the same time?

Thank God I still have my car.

I drove over to a coffee shop ten minutes away. Brandon was waiting for me. He made a show of tapping his watch. I was one minute late. Brandon was a punctual guy. Always had been. Always would be.

Brandon was also my best friend since kindergarten, so I knew I'd be forgiven easily. Otherwise, I might've gotten pissed at myself all over again for being late to a business meeting, even one minute.

All I could think about the whole drive over was Lake. I had to get her out of my goddamn head and focus.

"You're late, pussy."

We obviously liked to keep things professional.

"Christ, one minute." I shook my head at him.

Thank God I still had one good friend left. Most of them bailed on me, or went off and got married, had kids. They didn't want me around their spouses or children.

"You know how I am. You probably sat around the corner and waited to do it on purpose."

I snickered. "Actually, I really was one minute late."

Brandon stared at me for a while, long and hard. He sighed. "Who is she?"

"We're here for business."

"Your dick is distracting you, I can tell."

"Did you get the paperwork done?" Had to lure the conversation another direction, or he'd press for more information.

"All done." He slid some applications across the table.

"Thank you. This means a lot."

"It's no problem."

"Seriously, though. I couldn't do this without you."

It was true. Owning a business meant licensing. I needed his name on everything. It was my only shot. No way could I go to work for someone else. I'd had a taste of self-employment earlier in life, and it was all that drove me toward success now.

"You should've come to me the first time."

"I know." I couldn't look at him. I'd wanted to, but we were on different career paths.

"That guy was a fucking piece of shit." He lowered his voice and looked around for other patrons before dropping f-bombs. Brandon was cautious like that. A stand up dude. I owed him more than he knew.

I nodded.

"We should break his goddamn legs." Brandon's words

were for show. I didn't know if he even knew how to fight, but the sentiment meant a lot. He would if he had to. For me.

I'd do the same for him and he knew it.

"I'd rather just forget he existed. Ancient history."

Brandon's jaw ground together, and he nodded. "Okay."

I reached over and smacked him on the shoulder. "So, that's settled." I flashed him a smile, something I rarely did for anyone but him. I never thought I'd be the one trying to calm him down. Life is funny that way.

"Tell me about the girl."

I threw my hands up. "Come on, man." It was pointless to try and hide it from him.

"You really like her. I just got a smile."

I stared off at the wall and tried not think about what things would be like with Lake. It was impossible though. Goddamn, she was fucking smart, funny, and so hot. Images of her pussy clenching around my fingers floated through my mind. The way she gasped when I told her I wanted to fuck everything on her body.

"It's nothing. Can't happen."

"Why? They didn't take that away from you too, did they?" He grinned and pretended to look at my dick under the table.

Asshole.

"No, fucker. It's just—"

"Just what?"

"She's my step-sister's best friend."

"So. Sounds like one of those porn movies. My sister's best friend. My step-sister's hot mom."

"You done?" I tried not to laugh. He probably would've kept naming every porn trope in the book if I hadn't stopped him.

"Seriously, though. Why not? It's her friend. Not your sister."

"Baggage, man. She's smart, funny, going places."

"So are you." He returned the shoulder smack from earlier.

"I have nothing to offer her. She has a master's degree. She'll probably have to move to a big city. She deserves, well, someone like you." I waved a hand out to him. "Put together, has a career, money, 401k, that type of shit. I'm the gutter rat you make a mistake with before getting married."

His eyes narrowed. "At the risk of sounding like some Dr. Phil fuckbag…"

I laughed.

He sighed and shook his head. "Don't sell yourself short. Not this time."

I glanced up at him. Maybe he was right, but I still didn't buy into it. Not when it came to Lake. She should have the best of every fucking thing in the world. That included a man she could be proud of. That didn't have the kind of baggage I had floating around. And nobody could convince me otherwise of that. She was a fucking queen.

———

I went home. Whatever that meant. It wasn't really my home, but I had nowhere else to go. Excitement rushed through my veins as I checked a text on the way. I'd gotten the office space. Needed to take the landlord a check tomorrow. Easy enough. Things were clicking into place.

I walked through the front door. Lake sat on the couch in front of me. Cassie was next to her.

Fuck. Everything was going my way right then. I couldn't let her be a distraction. No matter what, I had to keep her away from me. Brandon always had his head in the clouds. He was a romantic, I was a pragmatist.

Lake's eyes brightened. Cassie frowned.

I walked past. Didn't want to disturb them. Just kept my eyes narrowed on the hallway. If I looked at Lake I might combust. I finally blew out a breath I'd been holding when I got to the hallway.

The sound of footsteps landed in my ear just as I was about to walk through to my room.

Her hand.

It grabbed me by the wrist. "Hey."

I spun around to face her. "Yeah?"

She frowned. It ate at me. All I wanted her to do the rest of her life was smile.

"Sorry. I just wanted to say thank you. For last night. I didn't get a chance to tell you, but I really appreciated it."

I glanced over at Cassie who glared from the couch, then back down at Lake. "Just be more careful next time."

I walked into my room and shut the door on her. Fuck, why was she making this shit so hard? Why'd she have to be there? I had to get out of this goddamn house.

———

Cassie and Lake didn't act like they were going anywhere anytime soon, so I snatched my checkbook and walked out. I'd get the guy's money early. Brandon would appreciate that. Good business etiquette.

Lake's eyes burned into the back of my skull as I stepped back out to greet the freezing-cold day once more. I still couldn't shake her, no matter how hard I tried. Hopefully, being a dick to her earlier would keep her away for a bit. I could go look for some apartments or houses to rent while I was out. Buy myself some time.

I took the long way over to the place I was going to rent for the business. Anything to buy some extra time, and let my cock settle down again. I stared down at my crotch. I was going to have to remedy the shit myself at some point in the near future.

I made my way over to the guy's office and wrote out a check. He had a small stack of papers on his desk. I handed over the check for the deposits and the first six months of rent. Just to make him happy and know I was reliable and had money to pay the bills. Hopefully, six months from now, the rent would be a drop in the bucket. Even with six months I had enough to conduct business and buy and sell things, until my profits could float all the expenses.

He pushed the papers over to me. "Paperwork. Need you to fill it out."

I thumbed through it. "Can I get this back to you tomorrow?"

"Sure."

"One other thing." I stared over at the picture of his family on the wall. He had four kids that were in the photo.

"What is it?"

"I have a partner. His name will be on most of this stuff. That okay? Do you need to meet with him?"

He eyed me cautiously. Like he was sizing me up at a poker table. "Why him?"

"Just business reasons."

He blew out a sigh and stared out the window this time..

"I swear, we're responsible. Legit. Please? I really need this, sir."

"You have credit problems?"

"No, nothing like that."

"I see."

Fuck me. What was he trying to get at? He had to be a sharp guy. I'm sure he'd figured it out by the way I fidgeted and practically begged.

"You won't have anything to worry about. I'll pay early every month after the six months. Hell, I'll pay the rest of the year at that time. In cash if you want it that way."

I looked him right in the eye. My entire career trajectory, at that time, depended on a landlord sitting three feet away.

"Nothing illegal goes in and out of those doors."

"Absolutely, sir. It's just office space and a place to meet with local clients. I'll list all the details and the business plan in here when I fill out the applications. I'll tell you whatever you want to know."

"You trying to make a better life for yourself?"

"Yes, sir."

"Good. We can make the arrangement then, so long as all your friend's info checks out."

A wave of endorphins ripped through my limbs. "Thank you. Seriously." I got up and shook his hand. "Thank you, sir."

"No problems."

"None." I got up and took a few steps toward the door. Then I turned around and faced him. "Why? Why are you helping me out?"

He stood up from behind his desk. Shoved both hands in his pockets and rocked back and forth on his heels. "I've sat in that same seat before. Down on my luck. Someone helped me out the same way."

I nodded my appreciation and turned around. Shoved the door open feeling like I could conquer the world.

"This check better clear."

I swear I heard him laugh as the edges of the door suctioned closed.

Two weeks had passed since I last saw Lake, and I was actually thankful for it. Everything was moving along with my business. I was set up, had licensing, had orders rolling in. It was perfect. Most of the time, I didn't even have to maintain an inventory, because I shipped the stuff straight from my suppliers to the customers.

Things were still rocky with the family, but it was what it was. When I wasn't working, I was in my room. I'd have enough saved up to rent an apartment soon. Then I could get myself out of the hell hole I lived in, and focus on making a living. I didn't have a meeting until later in the afternoon, and Cassie was out at a job interview.

It was just me and the house for the morning. I'd been working eighty hours a week and I figured I needed a morning off.

Just as I hit play on Netflix, the doorbell rang. Something always had to fuck with you right when you got comfortable. I knew it was too good to be true.

"Hang on!" I walked over and answered the door in nothing but my sweatpants, figured it was just someone selling something.

My heart leapt into my throat the second I opened the door.

Lake.

Fucking. Lake.

She'd gotten even hotter since the last time I saw her. At least it seemed that way. Maybe it was just being away from her so long.

Her eyes widened when she saw me shirtless. "Oh, hey. Umm, is Cassie here?"

My heart tried to pound its way out of my chest. I wanted to yank her into the house and make good on all my promises. My hand had been my only companion since I could remember, and I hadn't even had time for that with all the work hours.

I had to get her the fuck out of here before I made a mistake. "Job interview." I started to shut the door. It was rude as hell, but the longer it was open, the more dangerous the situation became.

"Oh. Okay." Her head dropped toward the ground and she turned.

My cock pointed north. So much so that I had to side-step a bit to keep it concealed. I shut the door, and immediately my head banged against it.

I watched Lake through the little square window at the top of the door. She took her time. I involuntarily head-butted the door once more, and my hand squeezed into a tight fist at my side. Her ass. Legs. Even with all the layers of winter clothes, I could still make out the curves of her tight body.

And sure, her body drove me crazy, but there was something about her too. She was strong, but shy. Head on straight. Interesting. Fuck, I could have a conversation with her. She had goals—ambitions.

"Don't sell yourself short."

Fucking, Brandon. His words fucked with my head. Was it me rationalizing why I could spend time with her? Just using it as an excuse to be close to her? Or were his words true?

Lake stopped on the steps when she heard my forehead beat on the door. She turned back, and I ducked out of the window, but I was almost positive she saw me.

Count to ten, motherfucker. Just let her go.

I got to three.

Couldn't take it anymore.

I had to have her. Even if it was just once. I wanted to feel her beneath me. Wanted to get this all out of my system. I was doomed.

Just as I'd started to get her out of my mind the last two weeks, she showed back up. It all erupted from somewhere deep inside my mind where I'd walled it all off.

I opened the door. She stopped, with her back still turned to me.

I walked out onto the porch. "Hey." It was safe on the porch. She wasn't in the house. I could do this, despite the fact I was freezing my nuts off.

She looked like she took a deep breath. Like she was fighting the same war in her own mind.

The cold sun cascaded around the sides of her head, and a few loose tendrils of hair around her ponytail glowed in the light. Finally, she turned back. Her hazel eyes burrowed into my skull, and rooted around in my brain, searching for something—information maybe.

"Hey."

"You want to hang out for a bit?"

"I don't know." She bit her lip and looked away.

I willed my cock to stand down, but he was having none of it. I stared around the neighborhood, hoping nobody else was out there. I'd walked out onto the porch without thinking about it but, fuck it.

Lake pretended not to notice, but I know she did.

"Are you here by yourself?" It was a normal question, but her eyes lit up in anticipation, like she was hoping for an answer.

I nodded.

She wiped her hands on her jeans. A subtle movement, but one I noticed. I could see it in her eyes. I could have anything I wanted from her, if I'd just take it.

"Come on." I nodded to the door.

She paused for another brief moment. Her hands trembled at her side. She was excited and scared at the same time. She knew what walking through that door meant. We damn sure weren't about to watch TV.

"Is anyone coming home any time soon?"

I narrowed my eyes to warn her that trouble was on the other side of that door, and I shook my head, slowly and deliberately. "Nope."

She gulped. But then she took a few steps toward the door.

When she passed by me, I said, "You sure?"

She didn't stop, just nodded slightly and went through the door.

I followed behind, trying to walk through at a normal pace, keep my cool. As soon as the door closed, a rush of euphoria greater than any drug ripped through my bloodstream, and I lost fucking control.

I fisted her ponytail and yanked her to my mouth. Our lips collided, and Lake moaned into my mouth. My free hand gripped her ass over her jeans, and I pushed her with my chest toward the couch, almost at a run. We fell into the sofa and I crashed on top of her. Hands, limbs, all tangled. I could barely breathe, couldn't think. All I could focus on was Lake touching me, kissing me.

All I wanted was my hands on her, everywhere at once. It was like starving in the desert, and then finding water.

I wanted to take her all in at once. Fuck taking my time. I wanted my cock inside her, wherever it would fit.

She pawed and beat at my chest, scratched my back, nearly to the point it looked like we were fighting. But her hands were hungry, her mouth, every bit of her body was on fire like mine.

I palmed one of her tits through the light sweater she had on and pinched her nipple as hard as I could, just to hear her gasp and squeal.

"Fuck, I've never done anything like this before." She panted the words at me.

"I told you what would happen."

"I want it." Her nails dug into my ribs so hard she had to have drawn blood. "Every fucking thing you said."

I ripped her sweater from her body. I didn't know how it came off and didn't care. It was shredded on the floor. Then I dug my fingers into her hips and flipped her over onto her stomach. Shoved her face down into the couch cushion while I worked my sweatpants off.

She tried to move up against my hand and I didn't let her.

"Oh my God."

Once my sweatpants were off, I fisted my cock. I kept my free hand on her head, shoving the side of her face into the couch cushion. I was so fucking hard, I didn't know how I'd last more than ten seconds inside her tight little pussy. "Never had a man fuck you any way he wanted?"

She blew out a huge breath. "God, no."

I smacked her on the ass over her jeans. She cried out and the moan that followed it was music to my fucking ears. My hand gripped her hair, and I pulled her mouth over to where I held my cock.

"Open up."

Her lips parted at my command and I shoved my cock down her throat. She gagged and coughed. Her eyes watered. My head flew back toward the ceiling. "Fuck, that's so good."

Once she grew accustomed to my dick in her mouth, her cheeks tightened around me. Her tongue swirled around my shaft. It was so euphoric, my hand relcased her head and I was outside of my body for a second. Everywhere and nowhere at once. Her mouth on my dick felt so goddamn good, I couldn't even speak or breathe for that matter.

I stared down at her eyes. They looked up at me while she sucked me off, bobbing her head as hard as she could. She watched every reaction on my face, like she was trying to learn what I liked.

I leaned back a little and thrust farther into her mouth, arched my back. "Fuck, Lake."

I bent down while she kept me in her mouth and massaged both of her ass cheeks. She was on her knees, bent over slightly, with her head cocked sideways. It was fucking perfect.

I yanked her jeans halfway down her legs, and she lifted her ass higher on instinct.

I spanked her again and felt her mouth tighten on my cock, and a whimper caught in her throat. Fuck her ass was so goddamn tight and beautiful. I wanted to bite the fuck out of it, just to see how it felt against my teeth.

"Are you wet for me?"

She nodded on my cock.

I ran a hand down her from behind to check. My middle finger slid right down the crack of her ass, and I pressed it against her tight puckered asshole. Her back arched and her muscles tensed at the sudden possible intrusion.

I circled the small ridges like I might shove my finger into it, but I didn't. "Soon." It was all I said, and her eyes grew large. "I want this pussy first."

She released me from her mouth and sucked in a huge breath. Her hand stroked across my wet cock, furiously. "Oh my God."

I palmed her slick cunt in my hand and worked it roughly back and forth. Circled her clit with two fingers and watched her eyes close at the sensation. It'd been a long time since I fucked a woman, and none of them had ever meant anything to me.

"It's so big." She eyed my dick while her hand worked from base to tip, over and over.

I shoved two fingers inside of her and a loud moan parted her lips.

"So fucking tight. Tell me what you want."

"God, fuck me, please."

"Can you take it all?"

Her head nodded, but her eyes had closed the second I put my fingers in her.

"Better make sure." I worked a third finger inside.

She gasped again.

I shoved her face back down into the cushion and dropped to my knees behind her. Yanked her around like she was nothing but a rag doll and lined her ass up in front of my face. I needed to buy some time, or my cock was going to erupt the second I shoved into her. I was pleasantly surprised I hadn't blown all over her hand and mouth already.

I buried my face into her hot cunt and gripped the front of her thighs hard enough to leave marks on her skin. My tongue flattened across her clit and her whole body squirmed while I held her in place. I sat there for a brief second, tongue pressed hard against her. Then I slid back, slowly and carefully, and dragged the tip of my tongue the length of her seam, barely parting her slick folds the whole way. Once I was past, I flicked my tongue across the sensitive skin between her pussy and her ass, and then worked my tongue around her asshole too.

She squirmed again and I gripped her legs tighter, holding her still. "You've never had anyone tongue your ass like this, have you?"

She shook her head. "God, you have the dirtiest mouth."

I smacked her on the ass again. The clap sound echoed off the walls.

"Fuck." The word trailed slowly off her lips.

I looked up over her ass, down the slender curve of her back, and up to her neck. Her face was pressed up against the side of the couch now. I couldn't take it anymore. Even if it lasted all of five seconds, I'd make it count. Then I'd fuck her again.

I lifted up and pressed the head of my cock against her clit from underneath. Her legs were forced together with her jeans tight around her thighs. I rocked my hips a few times to give some extra friction as my head slipped back and forth across her bundle of nerves.

I leaned over top of her, my mouth right next to her ear as I continued to tease her. "I'm sorry."

She frowned like maybe I was about to stop. "For what?"

"Just apologizing in advance for what I'm about to do to you."

I cupped a hand over her mouth and shoved into her hot pussy as hard as I possibly could. It was like fireworks going off inside of me. I saw brilliant flashes of black and red, and fuzzy stars filled my vision, just at the sensation of her pussy wrapped around my cock.

She screamed into my hand and then bit. I tilted her head back up to me, so that she was looking up toward the ceiling, and kept my hand locked around her mouth. My hips surged forward, and I drove my dick as deep as humanly possible into her. My free hand slid around her waist and I circled her clit with my fingers, fast and hard.

She moaned against my palm, and my mouth was still right next to her ear. "Say my fucking name when you come on my cock. And thank me for it."

My hand moved from her mouth and gripped her ponytail. I wrenched her hair up so that it was tight, and hammered into her pussy as hard and fast as I could. My hips crashed into her ass, and the wet, suctioning and smacking sounds filled the air around us.

I sped my fingers on her clit, and she looked like she tried to scream, but no words would come out. Her mouth was parted into an O, and nothing but labored breaths and moans escaped her lips.

"Gonna come on this dick?"

She nodded.

I tightened my fist in her hair and stroked my fingers back and forth on her clit, then fast hard circles. "Goddamn right you are, you dirty little bitch." I wrenched her head back up by her hair and then slid my other hand around her throat. Not hard enough to choke her, but hard enough that I could feel her heart beating against my fingertips.

Her legs and back and shoulders all tensed, and I could feel the waves of energy coursing up her back, and down through her arms and thighs. She started to tremble, which told me I needed to amp up the pace even more. I pistoned my cock in and out of her, the wet collisions growing louder and faster.

"Fuck. Fuck. Ohh, God Parker. Parker. Thank you, fuck." Her slick pussy cinched around my cock like a vise.

"Thank you, sir." I growled my words at her, and somehow managed to fuck her even harder. My grip moved from her throat to her collar bone, and I yanked her back into me, perfectly in time with each hard thrust.

"Th-thank you, s-sir." She barely got the words out as her whole body seized, and she came undone on my cock. Her hands fought to hold her body in the air, and I pulled her back up against my chest, and wrapped a forearm around her neck. My other hand still worked her clit in circles, and then back and forth as fast as my fingers could move.

Her hands slapped at my arm, and her nails dug into my forearms, and she seized up again right when the first orgasm had almost passed through her.

"Oh, you're naughty. You love that shit, don't you? Coming more than once, you greedy little bitch." I smacked her ass once more and she jolted and cooed her approval.

I palmed one of her tits, and it fit perfectly in my hand. The second orgasm rolled through her and she panted violently, and shoved her ass back against me, like she wanted more and more—couldn't get enough of my cock.

I pinched her nipple hard and twisted, then slapped the same hand across her other breast, like they were toys, put on earth solely for me to play with whenever I fucking wanted.

My balls started to tighten and lift, and I knew I wasn't going to last much longer. I didn't know where I wanted to come. Everywhere all at once.

"Oh my God, Parker, are you close?"

I smacked her ass again and smiled. "I'll tell you when I'm fucking ready. And I'll come wherever the fuck I want."

"Oh my God."

I bit down on her collar bone and shoved high and deep inside of her, like I was about to fill her pussy with every ounce of my come. Then I pulled out of her and threw her down on her back.

Instinctively, she pushed her tits together. It was so fucking hot, I thought I might lose it right there. I stroked my cock back and forth at the sight of it, then shoved between them. A fine sheen of sweat created the perfect amount of friction. God, fucking her tits was heaven. My load crept up my shaft, and I held it back as long as I could. My free hand gripped the ponytail on top of her head, and pulled her up so that her chin angled down toward her neck, so she could watch me blow my hot fucking load all over her.

The first wave came and shot across her tits and her hands that still cupped them together. Then I thrusted up to her mouth just in time for the second wave to blow all over her lips. Some of it ran across the sides of her mouth and on her chin. Then I buried my cock in her mouth and pulled her head forward onto me, while I grunted and rutted, releasing the very last bit. Her cheeks tightened on my shaft, and she used her tongue to milk every last drop from my cock.

I stood there, eyes wide, panting. Holy fucking shit. It was everything I'd dreamed it'd be, and more. Lake frowned when I walked off, but all I wanted to do was take care of her after what I'd just done. I'd been ridiculously rough with her. I think I was trying to chase her away, but she seemed to enjoy every second of it.

I went into the bathroom and got a towel and walked back out. She started to get up from the couch.

"No. Stay there."

She froze immediately at my words.

I wiped my come from her tits, hands, and her mouth. Then leaned in to kiss her on the lips. A soft, sensual kiss. Her breaths were still labored, and she just stared at me—watched me while I cleaned her up.

"Holy shit." Her words came out on a pant.

I leaned down and pressed my forehead against hers. "You okay?"

She nodded slightly against my head, and the corners of her mouth turned up into a smile.

It warmed my heart for the first time in probably ten years. The worst part was that we still couldn't be together. It had to be a one-time thing. And now, it was over.

Holy. Shit.

My brain was nothing but frayed, exposed wires. I couldn't think. Did that really just happen?

I'd never had an orgasm that intense in my life, let alone two in a row. The way he threw me around, gripped me with rough hands. It was even better than I'd imagined it would be, and he'd told me everything he would do to me.

I swear when it was over, he'd cracked a smile, looked on the verge of opening up to me, and giving me a little something of himself. There was more to him than what was on the surface.

And it was right then, that his face hardened right back into the Parker from before. His sentences shortened, and his tone switched back to assholish.

"I should, umm, get dressed."

He leaned back against the couch, and his eyes moved away from me.

I stood and slid my panties and jeans back up. My sweater was ripped in half and I held it up. He still didn't move or even try to look at me.

"I'll just grab something from Cassie's room."

Just say something, please.

He didn't. Just sat there while I walked away to the other room. I found a tee shirt and pulled it down over my head. My jacket would cover it up anyway. I stared in Cassie's mirror for a second. Fuck him, if he was going to be a jerk. I knew he had feelings for me, but I wasn't going to beg him to tell me. There was no way I was some booty call. I wouldn't be one, either, no matter how ridiculously good it felt to have him fuck me senseless and say the dirtiest things in my ear.

I took a deep breath and walked back out. He still sat there, staring off at the same spot on the wall. I grabbed my jacket. "I guess I'm going to go." I took a few steps toward the door with my tattered sweater gripped in my fist.

He leaned up. His eyes rolled over to mine.

Say something, asshole.

"You found a shirt. Good."

Are you fucking kidding me?

I ground my teeth together. "Yeah."

He stood up and walked toward me. Maybe I'd misjudged him.

"It can't be more than this."

Nope. Didn't misjudge him. His words sounded like the bullshit spewed from someone who used women for sex. I may have really liked him, like *really* liked him, but I wouldn't be made a fool of.

"Whatever." I turned the knob on the door.

He reached over and grabbed my forearm. Spun me around to face him.

"Don't make this harder than it has to be."

"You're the one making it difficult. You make everything difficult for yourself."

He sighed and moved his gaze toward the ceiling, then back to me. "I know."

"So stop doing it."

"It's not that easy. You wouldn't understand."

I nodded. "You're right. Because you won't tell me anything."

My fingers tightened around the sweater. We stared each other down for a few long seconds that felt like years. I could already feel myself wanting him to grab me and replay the entire scene from earlier. Butterflies landed in my stomach. I wouldn't do it though. I fucked him once to see what it would be like, but I wasn't going to do it again without some kind of knowledge there'd be more. That I'd get more from him than just sex.

"I'm trying to protect you. Keep you from making a mistake."

I put a palm on his cheek. His eyes softened for a brief moment, and he looked relaxed. "That's not your decision to make. And I'm not a woman you can just fuck when you feel like and then toss out of the house."

I went through the door before he could say anything else. It hurt. I had real feelings for him. More than I'd ever had for a man. But, I wouldn't lay my heart out there for someone who wouldn't do the same for me.

Everything but my love life was going as well as it could. It'd been two more weeks since the day Lake came over. I could still feel her touch, see her face everywhere. Even when my life was going great, it was still shitty. Maybe I was just cursed. Part of me thought our paths would cross, that she'd find some way to come to the house, just to see me. But, she didn't. She stayed away from me.

I unpacked the last two boxes in my new apartment. It was nothing special, a one-bedroom studio. But, it was mine. Revenue was coming in from the business, and I was meeting more people every day. New buyers. Hooking up with new suppliers. Everything was legit.

I actually had money to eat something other than Ramen noodles. I sat down on my futon couch and stared around at the room. This was just the beginning of my independence. I wouldn't fail. There was no way I could. I'd prove to myself and everyone else that I could still be successful.

What good was it all though, if I didn't have anyone to share it with?

There was a knock on the door.

What the fuck?

Maybe three people total knew where I was. My heart sped up with a quick burst, thinking maybe Cassie had told Lake. Maybe Lake had come over. It was stupid. I'd treated her like shit. I had to. Should've never let it go as far as it did.

It was Cassie instead. She had a box that looked like a new coffee maker in her hands.

I took it from her. "Come in. What are you doing here?"

"Wanted to bring you a house-warming gift. Figured you probably didn't get one from anyone else."

I gave her a side eye when I sat it down on the little breakfast bar that connected the living area and the kitchen. It wasn't like we were best friends, or even close for that matter.

"Your mom said it was your first place you've really lived on your own."

Fucking Mom. I didn't need her telling sob stories to people. I guess maybe she was proud of me in some weird way.

"Well thanks."

"Gotta have coffee, right?" She tucked her elbows into her palms like someone would do if they were cold, but I figured it was because she was uneasy.

"Yeah. It really will get some use. It's awesome." I walked over toward her and motioned for her to sit down.

I'd never talked to her like this before. It almost felt like we were family. I was afraid to ask anything about Lake. Wasn't sure what Cassie knew or didn't know, and if Lake would want anyone knowing about what happened with us.

"You looking for a reason to get out of the house, or what?"

"I don't know. It's weird."

"What is?"

"I got used to you being around all the time, and now you're not there anymore."

I chuckled. "You miss me, huh?"

"See, you're such an asshole all the time, that when you laugh a little, it's kind of awesome. People would probably like you if you weren't such a dick."

I sighed. "That sounded like a compliment."

Don't ask about Lake.

Cassie laughed. "I guess it was." She blew out a long breath. "I've never had a brother. So I guess it was kinda cool for a little while."

Don't ask about Lake.

"I mean, our parents are still married. Aren't they?"

"Yeah, I guess." She grinned.

"I really was worried about you two, the night at the club."

"You were worried about Lake. Don't fuck with me, Parker."

"Sure. You're right."

She frowned just a hint.

"But, I really was worried about you too."

"Really?" Her face snapped over to mine. "Don't lie, please."

I nodded. "I really was. Does your dad even know you're over here?"

"No."

Fuck me. If someone found out, I'd have to hear about it.

"Why?" she asked.

"Nothing. He just wouldn't want you here. I don't want any trouble."

"Why do you give a shit what he thinks?"

"I don't want any problems for my mom. She'll have to hear about it."

"What did you do that was so bad? He warned me about you like you were a serial killer or a terrorist or something."

"I really don't want to talk about it."

She nodded. I was surprised she gave up that easy. Most people didn't.

Don't ask about Lake.

"How's Lake?" *Nice self-control, Parker.*

"Good. She's been really busy the past few weeks; going on job interviews, apartment hunting in the city. I've barely gotten to hang out with her at all."

"Sorry."

"It's cool. I'll find someone for her. God, she needs to get laid. She works way too hard."

My jaw clenched, and I was pretty sure every muscle in my body squeezed so tight that I trembled. Heat rushed into my face.

Cassie glanced up. The look I made must have been pretty apparent.

She held her hands up. "God, man. I won't find someone for her."

I sighed.

"Why don't you tell her how you feel? I'm pretty sure she'd fall right into your arms."

"I can't. And no, she wouldn't. She'd be too afraid of pissing you off."

"Whatever." She stood up. "I gotta go."

"Okay." I got up and walked her over to the door. Couldn't help but think I kind of liked Cassie, in a brother-sister kind of way. It was unexpected, but I'd been kind of lonely and it was nice of her to come by. "Thanks again. For the coffee maker. It really will get put to use."

Then she did something I hadn't expected. She hugged me.

"Tell her how you feel. I know I was a dick before, but I really think maybe you're good for her. I don't care what my dad said. You seem like a decent guy to me. She's throwing herself into finding a job and an apartment right now. I know it's because of you. That's how she gets."

"I'll think about it."

"Please really do that. I really don't want to see her sulk around during Christmas. It's like her favorite thing ever."

"Okay, I'll think about it."

"Okay." Cassie walked out the door.

It wasn't going to happen. I shouldn't have slept with Lake. I'd already hurt her enough. She needed to get over me. Hopefully, she'd find her dream job and move to a different city soon. It sucked a bag of dicks, but it was the way it had to be. It was what was best for her.

Two weeks and he hadn't tried to call or find me. Got what he wanted, and that was it. Oh well. I wasn't going to sit around and pine after him. He still invaded every thought, but I refused to let him hurt me.

I stalked through my parents' kitchen with purpose. Getting a job or finding an apartment was priority number one. Parker could sit around and feel sorry for himself and lament his big secret past that ruined his life on his own time. I didn't have time for that kind of shit. I had a world to conquer, and I wanted it all wrapped up with a pretty bow before Christmas, so I could enjoy that time with my family.

Cassie walked in. She never knocked on the door. "Another job interview?"

"Yeah." I turned to her. "I'm excited about this one. It's a big-time design firm in Chicago."

"You look real excited."

I tried to plaster a fake smile on my face. How much had Parker fucked with me?

"I'm serious."

"Do you even take time to breathe? I've barely even seen you."

"I'm sorry. I just have to get out of—" I waved a hand around at the house. "This."

"Have you talked to him?"

"Who?"

"Don't treat me like I'm an idiot."

My heels screeched on the tile when I stopped abruptly. "No. Don't plan on it either."

"What happened?"

I stared at her. Couldn't lie to my best friend. "I liked him. We hooked up once. Haven't seen him since. I'm sorry. I shouldn't have—"

"Don't worry about me. I know him about as well as you. It's not like you banged an actual brother of mine."

I gave her a look that said *really?*

"I'm serious. Don't give a shit. Just want you to be happy."

"I am happy."

"You don't look it."

"Okay. Maybe I wanted more. But he didn't, and I don't have time to wait for him to figure things out. And he doesn't need to decide what's best for me to know and not know." I walked to the counter and picked up a cup of coffee. "I don't need a man to act like my parent. I want a partner. And he's not it."

A sly grin spread across Cassie's face and she walked over and sat down in a chair. "So, what happened?"

"God, you're such a gossip."

"Shut up and tell me, bitch."

I shook my head and took a sip of the coffee. "You're not going to let this go, are you?"

"Oh no."

"Fine." I was in a hurry, and she wasn't going to leave until she knew. So, I told her everything.

"Holy. Shit."

I realized I was grinning a little for the first time in two weeks, just reliving all of it. "Yeah." I still had goosebumps thinking about everything Parker did to me in their living room. Could still feel his powerful fingers digging into my hips, and his hand on my head, shoving me down into the couch.

"I don't know if I'll ever look at him the same in my house now."

My fingers squeezed tight around the coffee mug at the thought of Cassie looking at him at all. What had he turned me into?

"So, what are you going to do?" Cassie asked.

My eyes rolled over to her. "What do you mean?"

"I mean, holy hell, I had to fan my face just now. That's rare. You have to make him come after you."

I shook my head. "No. He makes me insane."

"Don't you wonder what his big secret is?"

"Don't care anymore."

Cassie snickered.

"I don't."

"Sure."

I glanced up at the clock. "Oh God."

"What?"

"I have to go."

"Fine. But hang out with me soon. I miss you."

I sighed. "Okay, promise."

We walked out the door and to our cars together. Cassie gave me a big hug. "Kick ass at your interview."

"I will."

"He has an apartment now. Let me know if you want to know where it is." She waggled her eyebrows at me.

"I don't."

"Mmhmm." She walked off to her car.

It was good to know that Parker was getting his life in order, but I didn't need to know any more than that.

If he had his own place, I could go over there, and he could fuck me all he wanted and we'd never have to worry about being caught.

Pull yourself together.

I shook my head at myself in the rearview mirror. What was he doing to me? Surely it would end sometime. If he wanted me, he'd have come after me already.

———

Indianapolis was a few hours away from Hope. I walked out of the interview feeling confident as hell. I'd killed it. I just knew it. The only thing was that I'd have to move there. It's where their main offices were, and it was longer than anyone would want to drive every day to commute. Everything I'd seen at the interview pointed to the fact the job was pretty much mine. They were looking for a staff-level hire they could mold into a senior partner over time.

I was lighter than air when I floated into my car. I stared at all the Christmas lights and decorations as I drove through the city. Everything was brighter, happier.

When I got back to Hope, I stopped off at the grocery store to pick up a few things I'd promised my mom. She wanted to make dinner to celebrate yet another job interview. It was sweet, but she made a big production of it and I'd been on approximately five interviews in the past seven days.

I parked the car and snagged a cart on the way in. The town was just big enough that you didn't know someone everywhere you walked, but it was common to run into someone you knew from childhood or school. My second grade teacher, Mrs. Harden, pushed a cart in front of me.

We were exchanging hellos by the produce section upon walking in when I saw it. A flash of black did a U-turn and hauled ass around the corner. *Please, God, no.*

My feet were moving before I could stop them. Just left Mrs. Harden and her conversation in the dust. It was Parker. I knew it was.

So many questions flashed through my mind. Why hadn't he called? Why hadn't he talked to me? What was his problem?

I told myself I didn't care. My mind seemed on board with that. But, my feet apparently wanted to get to the bottom of the situation.

I steered around the corner and there he was, reaching up for a can of something, pretending like the rest of the world didn't exist. Like he hadn't just bolted the second he saw me. And God, he was as beautiful as ever. Levi's that sculpted his ass just right. His black V-neck tightened around his bicep as he pulled the item down and pretended to examine it.

I faked a cough.

He sighed, and his head dropped. "Hi."

Hi? Hi? Is he kidding me?

"How's it going, *Parker?*"

His stare remained angled to the ground. "I'm sorry."

"For what exactly?" I wasn't about to make this shit easy on him.

He turned slowly to face me and there actually appeared to be some pain in his eyes. I folded my arms across my chest. I had on a mid-length black skirt, heels, and a white button-down blouse. I looked hot as hell and planned on making him see every inch of me.

Parker blew out another long breath. Didn't say anything else.

My jaw tightened. No way was he going to give me the silent treatment right now. I walked up next to him. "What are you sorry for?"

He just stared at me. We stood there deadlocked. The longer he went without saying anything, the more heat rushed into my face. Still, nothing from him. Fuck that. He wasn't worth my time.

"You're an asshole." My hands gripped the cart and I took off with a few quick steps.

To hell with it. I didn't need an explanation from him. I was on my way out of this town anyway.

"Wait."

Don't stop for him. Don't.

I stopped, but somehow managed enough self-respect to keep my back to him. I squeezed my eyes shut and then opened them again. I felt like I might cry, and I didn't cry for anyone. Why was I so upset about this anyway?

"What do you want?" The words came out hateful.

I heard him take a couple steps in my direction. Heard was an understatement. I could feel them in my legs, and the vibrations crept up my spine. I couldn't tell if it was in a good way or bad way, probably a little of both. The sounds echoed off the linoleum floors and up to the high ceilings.

"Trying to do what's best for you."

I shook my head. This guy and his macho bullshit. "I can decide what's best for myself. I don't need you to do it for me."

"Yeah, this time you do."

I whipped around. My face was a glowing ember, each breath just stoking the flames higher. "You're a prick."

He smirked. He smirked right at me. "Yeah, I am."

"Go to hell." I tried to walk away, but he grabbed me by the arm. Not forcefully, but enough to make me stop.

I whipped back around to him. "What?"

It happened.

Before I knew it.

His lips collided with mine.

I don't know what came over me. She was pissed off and I just wanted to make her happy. We abandoned both carts in the middle of the aisle. I hoisted her up and carried her to my car. Sped the whole way to my apartment, praying she wouldn't change her mind.

It was bad. I shouldn't have been doing it. I should've been pushing her farther away, not dragging her straight into my life. I didn't want to ruin everything she had going for her. But, I couldn't stop myself.

We crashed through the door to my new apartment and I kicked it shut behind me. She backed away a few steps and stared at me with half-hooded eyes.

"Tell me your secret."

I shook my head. "Don't."

She backed a step toward the bedroom door. "Tell me."

I stalked toward her. Her pulse sped up on her neck and her eyes were fully dilated. It took everything I had to control myself. I wanted to scream it at her. Get everything off my chest, the weight off my shoulders, but I couldn't do that to her.

She took another step back into the doorway.

I raked my gaze up and down her body. That fucking skirt and her brunette hair curled down to her shoulders. My cock was so hard I thought I might pass out.

"I want to know."

I backed her into the bedroom and turned her up against the wall, so that we were nose to nose. "Don't."

She started to say something, and I gripped her blouse and yanked it open. Button shrapnel pelted the walls and a black, lacy bra corralled her tits. I shoved my chest into her and cupped one in my palm.

"Oh my God." Lake gasped the words.

My hands slid down her hips and I gripped the hem of her skirt and yanked it up over her ass. I didn't know who I was around her. Everything about Lake. Her intensity. Her feisty attitude. I couldn't control myself.

"You don't know what you fucking do to me." I growled the words in her ear.

"I can't—"

I bit down on her neck just as she began to speak. Her sentence turned into a jumbled gasping of air.

"You're going to get hurt."

Her hand found my cock. "Don't care."

My eyes rolled back when she stroked my shaft over my jeans.

I fisted her hair and shoved her down to her knees. All I could think about was my cock in her mouth. The memory of how well she sucked my dick back at the house played through my mind.

The second I pulled my jeans down she lunged forward and wrapped her lips around me by surprise.

Fuck!

I beat my fist on the wall it felt so fucking good. Part of it got my blood boiling even more, her taking control like that. Like some of my power had been taken. But, as I stared down at her eyes, I didn't give a fuck. It felt too damn good. She released me from her lips for a brief moment, enough to suck in a couple of deep breaths, and then took me damn near to the base.

Her eyes turned glossy and her face was flushed with pink hues, but she didn't stop.

I finally grabbed her under her arms and pulled her up to her feet. "You want to be a naughty little bitch again?"

She grinned slightly and nodded.

I hauled her over to the bed and pushed her chest down into it, leaving her ass high and exposed. Her black skirt was bunched up around her waist. I spanked her on the ass, hard. Enough to leave a pink hand print. She let out a squeal, followed by a purr.

"Didn't get enough of this last time, huh? Came back for more?" I smacked her again, this time on the other cheek.

All she could do was nod against the bed. I cupped her hot cunt in the palm of my hand and leaned down into her ear.

"You like when I take what's mine?" I squeezed her hot pussy and circled her clit with my index finger.

"Uh huh." She moaned the words. Her breaths came hard and fast like I could command them with my fingers.

I shoved two fingers inside, forcefully. I angled them to hit the spot deep inside of her, and pistoned my fingers in and out. She was so damn hot her wetness was trailing down to my wrist.

Her fingers gripped the bedsheets and I continued to say anything I wanted in her ear.

"You want me to fuck you again?"

"God, yes, please."

"Why should I?"

"Because I need you inside me."

Fuck, her words were going to get me off before I even got my dick wet. I placed a hand on her head and shoved up off her. Pulled my fingers out of her at the same time. Her body tensed up and her ass jolted back, like she wasn't done being finger-fucked yet.

I took my time, admiring her ass, and her swollen pink entrance. I wanted to fuck her so bad, but it was worth it to take my time and tease her. It was a lot of fun watching her squirm too.

"Look at this here." I spread her ass cheeks and bent down. Admired both of the holes I wanted to fuck. I teased my tongue around the rim of her ass, then pressed it flat against her pussy and licked it from top to bottom.

"God, I'm so close."

I gave Lake another quick swat. "Don't come until I tell you."

"I don't need your permission."

Goddamn, I loved how sassy she was. I stood up behind her and shoved my cock up against her pussy, just enough to let her feel how close it was, and then leaned down over her back. "If you want this dick, you'll do as you're told."

She started to smart off again and I teased the head of my dick around her clit. Her legs stiffened and her back arched. "Fine, I won't come yet. Just fuck me, please. I need it."

I let my head and shaft glide back and forth beneath her. I could feel the heat radiating from her with each stroke.

"Please," she begged.

I flipped her over so that she was on her back. I wanted to watch her face as I went into her. Her eyes widened with surprise when she landed. I hadn't meant to be that rough, but I wanted my cock inside her just as bad as she wanted it.

Her legs immediately spread, an open invitation.

I grinned.

"Give it to me."

I threw both of her feet up to my shoulders and stared down at her. Then I slapped my cock on top of her clit, just to watch her squirm a little more.

"Oh my God." Her eyes rolled back.

"So needy."

"Mmhmm."

I leaned down and put my hand over her mouth. Stared into her eyes. Then I shoved in as deep and as far as I could go.

Sparks of electricity shot through my limbs, from my balls all the way through my arms and legs. Euphoria radiated through me, straight up my spine and through my extremities. Nothing in the world felt like being inside Lake. It was like a spiritual experience.

And as soon as my cock was inside her, I only wanted more. Deeper, faster, harder—she was a drug, and I wanted to overdose on it.

My arms wrapped around her legs and I started yanking her into each one of my thrusts, until I was rutting like a wild animal. Her arms flew back on the bed and her hands clawed frantically at the sheets.

Her tits were still inside the bra, but I fucked her so hard they came out and bounced back and forth.

"Oh my God. Oh my God."

I slid a hand down and thumbed her clit while I pumped in and out of her.

The wet suctioning sounds of my cock hammering in and out of her echoed off the walls and intermingled with gasps, heavy breathing, and moans. The headboard thumped against the wall like a drumbeat. I didn't care. Didn't give one fuck about who heard, or how loud it was, or if anything was breaking. I just never wanted to not be inside her.

"I can't—"

I could see in Lake's face that she was in agony, holding back her orgasm.

"You want to come on my cock?"

"Y-y-yes, p-please."

"Not yet."

"Fuck you."

"Oh, I'm definitely doing that." My hips sped up and my finger circled her clit as fast as I could go.

"Please, Parker." Her syllables lingered in the air.

"Okay. Come on my dick, *now*." I drilled into her as fast and hard as possible. The neediness in her voice only made my cock harder. Her moans turned into a silent gasp, like she was trying to scream, but the words wouldn't come out. Her toes curled against my cheeks and her whole body quivered.

Her tight cunt squeezed around my cock like a vise, so damn hard I got lightheaded.

"Goddamn." I kept myself buried to the hilt, as far as I could go. Just stayed deep inside her and focused on the sensations of her greedy, slick walls spasming around my shaft, pulling me into her.

Her orgasm rolled through her limbs in huge waves, and her hands pawed at the sheets.

"Oh my God, Parker. Parker—"

"I love when you say my name while you come."

After a few more convulsions, she finally relaxed. Her back had been arched, and it slammed down into the bed. I pulled out of her before I blew my load.

She sat there for a brief second, appearing to collect her wits about her. I climbed up onto the bed and rolled onto my back next to her, then grabbed her by the hips and shoved her up on top of me.

"Get on top." It was a forceful command.

Her eyes lit up like she'd been waiting for this opportunity. My cock pointed straight toward the ceiling, and she straddled it.

She teased my head around her entrance, and I gave her a quick swat to the ass.

"Ride it."

She lowered herself onto me and my head turned to fuzz again. Fuck, there was nothing like being inside of

Lake's cunt. I could've lived the rest of my life fucking orgasms out of her.

She leaned down to kiss me, and I bit her lip. She yelped.

"I said fuck me."

Her hips rolled back and forth on me, slow at first, and then steadily grinding harder and faster.

She bit her lip and pawed at her hair.

It was the hottest fucking thing I'd ever seen in my life. I laced my fingers behind my head and let her have her way with me for a bit. Just watched her.

Her tits began to bounce harder and faster, and she was already working toward another orgasm. She'd roll her hips in slow circles and then bounce, all in the same steady rhythm.

"Bounce on it again."

She did what I told her. Began to spring up and down and I looked down and watched my cock going in and out, disappearing then reappearing.

"Rub your clit while you fuck me."

She didn't even think about it. Her hand just shot down to her pussy and her fingers played back and forth across it. She looked like she was about to come again, and I smacked one of her breasts, just to watch it fly back and forth. Then I tweaked one of her hard nipples.

She let out a squeal once more, followed by a purr.

"Not yet. Beg me for it."

She could barely even speak, but she tried anyway. Her words came out through gritted teeth. "You just love torturing me, don't you?"

"You bet your fucking ass I do."

I gripped both of her hips and dug my fingers in, then shoved her down onto me, each time with more force than the last. Her brunette hair hung down and framed her gorgeous face.

Her blouse still hung loosely from her shoulders and her bra clung to her skin beneath her tits. I grabbed her shirt and pulled it off. She read my mind and unclasped her bra and tossed it to the floor. Must not have wanted me to tear it off her, which was what was about to happen.

"God, your cock feels so good."

"Oh yeah?" I gave my hips a quick thrust and got a moan in response.

"God, yes."

"You want me to fuck you harder?"

She nodded and bit her lip.

"You want me to pin your arms behind your back and fuck that pussy the way you need it?"

"Mmhmm."

"All you have to do is ask, Lake."

"Please, God, yes."

I gripped both her forearms and wrenched them behind her back, then yanked her chest down into me. She let out another squeal.

"Oh my God."

Her hard nipples pressed against my chest, and I lifted onto the balls of my feet.

"You asked for this." I slammed my cock into her, over and over.

I fucked her so hard and our slick, wet skin smacked like a round of applause.

She tried to scream out, but it only sounded like a stutter.

"Oh-oh-oh my-my-my fu-fu—"

I held her wrists with one hand and fisted her hair with the other.

"Where do you want me to come?"

She couldn't even respond, and my balls had already lifted and grown tight. I slammed up into her and pulled her down onto me at the same time. She squirmed under my grip until she couldn't hold out any more.

"Fuck, Parkerrr!"

She clenched that pussy around me once more and my cock kicked. We came in tandem, and I blew my hot load into her cunt while she spasmed on top of me. I thrust once more with another intense wave, as my whole body tingled from head to toe, starting at the base of my spine.

For a brief second, our bodies both locked up, nothing but tense muscles, joined together as close as two people can possibly be.

I looked up into her eyes at that moment, and it was just —right. Everything was right in the world when I came inside her. The first time was intense, and rough, and fantastic, but something had been missing.

I didn't want to move. Didn't want to breathe. Didn't want the moment to end. She was marked. She was *mine*.

Eventually, life rushed back into both of us, and we sat there, chests pressed together, lungs searching the room for oxygen.

"You came inside me." She said it almost like a question.

I nodded. A primal part of me loved that I'd done it. For a quick moment, I thought about what it'd be like if she got pregnant. What it'd be like to watch her carrying my child—taking care of her, taking care of both of them. It was just a fantasy, but it was one that made me want to smile.

Our foreheads pressed together. Regret started to creep back in, maybe on both our parts.

"Fuck it, I don't care." Her lips pushed against mine.

I tasted her berry lip gloss.

"God, you're beautiful." I wasn't usually one for giving compliments or saying shit like that. I think it was unexpected for her. It was like a glimpse at the old me, and her lips curled into a smile.

"Thank you," she whispered.

We sat there, staring at each other for what seemed like an eternity.

What was I doing? What was all of this?

It wasn't my style. He wasn't my type. But I couldn't quit.

I was almost positive I'd get the job offer, and I'd have to move away, and yet something inside of me told me that if a relationship with Parker was possible, I'd give it all up. He was all I thought about. He consumed me. It was stupid. I barely knew him, but there was just something about him. If he'd just open up to me.

Think, Lake. Fuck.

I needed to be an adult. Find out where this was going. I needed to know more about him. We hadn't even been on a date and we'd already screwed twice. It was so unlike me.

"What are we doing?"

Parker's eyes met mine. He shook his head. "I don't know."

"Parker."

"Yeah?"

"I can't keep doing this. Feeling like this."

Parker sighed and looked away. "I'm sorry."

"What do you want from me?"

"I don't know."

"Well, can we try to figure this out?"

His eyes came back to meet mine. "This is why I told you to stay away from me."

"You think I knew you were in the grocery store? I've been trying."

"I know. It's just—"

I got up from the bed. He had that look in his eyes, that guarded look about him again. I didn't need to ask questions to know I wasn't going to get any answers. I started putting my clothes back on.

"Where are you going?"

"Staying away. It's what's best, remember?"

"I didn't mean—" He scrubbed a hand through his hair. "Didn't mean you have to leave this second."

"Why? It's not like you're going to tell me anything anyway."

He sat up in bed while I searched for my skirt. "It's not like that. I'm trying—"

I whipped around to face him. "What? Trying to protect me?"

"Yes."

Heat rushed into my face and both of my hands balled into fists. "I don't need to be protected. I just want to be with you. I want to know whatever is eating you alive every day. And for some reason you think you know more about what I need than I do."

"Maybe I do."

I shimmied my skirt up my hips and glared. "Maybe you don't." I started for the front door. I couldn't help but think maybe I was madder at myself than Parker, for letting myself feel this way again—to be hurt. Even though I knew exactly what would happen if I'd come over. It was my fault, so I just wanted out of his apartment.

I started through the door and somewhere in my own thoughts I'd lost track of what he was doing.

Footsteps stormed behind me. I reached for the door handle and a big, rough palm slapped over it before I could get to it.

"You want to know everything? Huh?" His words weren't a shout, but they were laced with controlled anger.

To hell with him. I wouldn't back down to his wannabe show of manhood, or whatever this was. "I did. Not anymore."

"What *did* you want to hear?"

"Nothing. Move your hand and let me out."

"No. You want to know everything. Tell me what you want to know. Tell me you can handle it."

"I could have. I don't want to anymore."

Part of me wondered why I was fighting him now. I wanted him to tell me, but not like this. I wanted him to tell me things because he wanted to. I wanted him to trust me with whatever secrets he had. I didn't want to beat it out of him or manipulate him into it.

"No. You said you wanted to know. All my big dark secrets."

"I don't want to have to piss you off to get answers out of you, Parker. I want to tell you things. You could ask me anything and I'd tell you."

"Oh, really? Really?"

"Yes."

"Are you going to take a job and move away?"

My heart dropped into my stomach. "Maybe."

"Bullshit, you know you will."

"How did you know I was going to take a job somewhere else?"

"Oh, you mean, you can have secrets, but I can't?"

My jaw clenched tight. "I haven't been offered a job yet. And you haven't been talking to me. Otherwise, you'd have known."

"Whatever."

"Move your hand. I'm not going to stand here and do this all day."

"I can't."

My eyes snapped up to his. "Can't what? Is your hand stuck like that on the door?"

"I can't let you leave."

Something about his words, his tone. It sent my heart racing. I hated him even more for it. How did he do this to me? How did he manipulate all my emotions, through the whole spectrum, so easily? Already, I wanted him to just grab me and carry me to the bedroom again. The weird thing was part of me didn't want him to tell me whatever his secrets were either. The whole mystery, and angst of not knowing, made me somehow drawn to him even more.

"Why?"

His eyes darted around the room and landed back on me. "Watching you walk away hurts too much."

He dropped his hand from the door and walked back through the room. Right past me.

I stared down at the door handle. Walking through the door was the right move. It was what I should do. Go get my dream job. Move to the city. Forget that Parker even existed.

I closed my eyes and then opened them again. Took a deep breath.

I reached for the knob and turned it, then took a step out into the daylight.

Parker stood behind me. I couldn't see him, but somehow, I knew he still had his back turned and wasn't looking at me.

"I was in prison."

My heart squeezed.

PARKER

S he froze up. Stopped right in her tracks.

Fuck.

Why did I tell her? The words just came out and I couldn't stop them. There was no way she'd understand. Nobody ever did. She would look at me with nothing but pity and disgust from that moment forward, I just knew it.

She just stood there. Why wasn't she moving?

"There, now you know the truth. You can get on with your life. Go find someone that's not a felon. Have a fairytale of a life with two kids in a suburb, and leave the degenerates where they belong."

Lake turned around, slowly. A tear streamed from one of her eyes. "What'd you do?"

"What do you care?"

She started back through the door. I didn't know what she expected. What could she say? She needed to leave and get the fuck away from me.

"I do care. What'd you do? I want to know."

I looked away. "It doesn't matter. It is what it is."

She walked right up to me. Then she took me by surprise. She shoved me. "What'd you do?"

"You should go."

"Tell me."

Another shove. They came one after the other until I was backed up against a wall in my living room.

"Why do you care?"

"Because I want to know what you did that's so horrible that I can't be with you. That'd make you fuck me and then throw me away like garbage."

I held my hands up. "It's not like that. Please—"

"It *is* like that, Parker. You can roll around in bed with me but then, oops, time to go. Nothing more than that."

"I killed a guy, okay? Is that what you want to hear?" My words echoed off the wall. I didn't realize how loud I'd shouted it. I'd probably be evicted within the week.

Lake's eyes widened. "What?"

"I saw a man abusing a woman and I hit him. He cracked his head on the pavement. He died. The woman said I attacked him for no reason. Denied it all. I was charged with manslaughter. I made a plea deal, so I wouldn't end up stuck in prison my entire life."

She backed up a few steps. Her chest heaved up and down, like she was having a panic attack. "Sorry, I didn't—"

I looked away. I hadn't even said it out loud since I'd left prison. My jaw tightened, and my stomach roiled. That one fucking night. That asshole beating on his girlfriend. I shouldn't have even been there. My business was just starting to take off, and then my whole life was snatched away from me. Now, I had to get all my business licenses in my best friend's name, just to make a living. My last partner stole all my clients and all the money we'd made.

I had to start over with nothing when I got out.

I hadn't meant to kill the guy that night. I was just trying to keep him from hitting that woman one more time. I'd tried to reason with him at first, and he took a swing at me. I just reacted. So stupid. That's what was fucked up about the world we lived in. You try to help someone, and you end up getting hurt.

But it was no excuse. Lake had a life to live still, and I wasn't going to fuck it up for her.

She walked toward me.

"Don't. Just go, Lake."

She shook her head. Put her hands on my shoulders and stared at my face. "I know you'd never hurt anyone on purpose."

"You don't know that." Maybe it was true at one time, but not now. Ten years I spent in prison. It changed me. I had no qualms about hurting anyone now. People were just put on earth as means for others to use to get what they wanted, nothing more. Nobody meant anything to anyone.

"Yes, I do. You're not a bad person."

I glared back at her, met her eyes. "Yeah, I am. Now please go, before I get upset."

"You don't mean that."

My words came through gritted teeth. "Yeah. I do."

More tears rolled down her cheeks and dropped to the floor. She shook her head. "Tell me you want me to leave. And I'll leave."

I stared her in the face. The most beautiful face I'd ever seen. Of course, I didn't want her to leave. I wanted to be with her more than anything in the world. I wanted to grab her and hold her and protect her. I didn't want her to ever hurt. It would only prolong the inevitable though. Somehow, maybe not today, or tomorrow. But, somewhere down the road, my past would hurt her. *I* would hurt her. It was better to cut it off now when it was still just an infatuation. I had nothing to offer that was remotely good enough for her. I was holding her back.

My throat was dry as a desert, and I nearly choked on the words, but managed to get them out. "I want you to leave."

Her eyes narrowed. She sniffled, like she was trying to keep from crying more at my expense. "Fuck you."

And she walked out my front door.

LAKE

"I'll take it."

My palms were slicked with sweat as I clutched the cell phone in my hand. My legs were nothing but Jello.

Still, for the past week, all that'd been on my mind was Parker. I'd gone back for a final interview at the design firm in Chicago. They'd loved me even more than the first time, so it seemed.

Parker.

His name and face still played through my head. Fuck him. He'd told me to leave. I tried to understand where he was coming from, but part of me wondered if he'd given me the real story. I knew him. I'd seen his expressions soften, the weaker sides of him come out. There was no way he was capable of actual murder, but murderers were always people you didn't expect.

In my brain, I told myself to run. It was safe. He wasn't worth the risk. But part of me thought a man's life shouldn't be ruined, tarnished, over something he'd done in the past. Especially if he was innocent or had tried to help someone else.

My God, if that was true, if he was telling the truth. It had to be hell for him. Ten years in prison. The prime years of his life.

"Hello? Lake?"

I shook my head and snapped out of my daze. "Yeah, sorry."

"When can you start?"

Such a simple question. And yet, I sat there and debated the answer back and forth. Parker wasn't coming for me. He'd shoved me away. I understood why he did it, but did he think I was that shallow? That I couldn't make my own decision on the matter? Facts were facts, though. He'd made up his mind about me, and I couldn't do anything about it. You can't force someone to love and trust you.

"As soon as possible."

"Okay, we'll be in touch. Can't wait to have you."

The line went dead, and I tossed the phone on my bed. I fell back into my pillow and let out a huge breath, mentally exhausted.

But it wasn't from the new job, or the new life change. It was Parker. That stupid, beautiful, stubborn face of his.

Every scenario with him played in my head over and over. He turned me into a different person. A person I didn't even know. How could I ever be with another man, when I knew that he was out there somewhere? The thought of him with any other women sent my hackles rising.

I wanted him. He didn't want me, for stupid reasons. That was the biggest thing. I'd tried to think if I could get past all of it, and I was lying to myself if I thought it'd be easy. That love would just conquer whatever and I'd just forget all about his past. That worried me more than anything. I knew I'd struggle with it, and I shouldn't, if he was telling the truth.

A knock at the door had me sitting upright in the bed. I got up and walked through the hallway and to the front door.

Part of me couldn't help but get excited about the fact that maybe I'd open the door and see him.

But, I didn't. It was Cassie, the next best thing, I supposed.

"Bitch."

She said the word, but it wasn't the same. Nothing was the same anymore. I could already feel the feelings rushing up to the surface. My face heated, and butter-flies swarmed my stomach.

I couldn't even speak. Just held the door open and she walked by.

Cassie knew me. The second she turned around, I turned into a puddle. She'd instinctively already reached out to catch me in a hug.

"I'm sorry." Her hand stroked through my hair.

I burst into tears. "I got the job."

It was supposed to be a happy moment, and it was the worst. I wanted to tear down the walls and throw things. My heart was shattered because the man I loved had tossed me out of his apartment. Didn't want anything to do with me.

Nothing hurts like love.

"Oh, sweetie."

She didn't try to tell me it was a good thing, or that I'd get better. That was the thing about Cassie. That was why we were best friends. She knew me.

She knew I'd pick myself up after a while, and forge on like I always had.

"Come on. Let's sit down." She led me over to the couch.

I sniffled and tried to get rid of the tears and hold myself together.

"I told them I can start as soon as possible."

Cassie nodded. "Okay."

PARKER

P ounding.

On my door.

What the fuck?

I pulled myself off the couch and walked over. The fist didn't stop. Shit was rattling on the walls and my teeth started to grind. "Hey, knock it off!" I yanked the door open.

Cassie exploded right at me, like a pouncing cat, as soon as I opened the door. She shoved me backward. "What the fuck, Parker?"

I wasn't sure I'd ever seen her so angry, even the night she was drunk at that club. In fact, I wasn't sure I'd ever seen *anyone* so angry, and I'd been to prison, for fuck's sake.

She shoved me again.

"What the hell? Stop pushing me."

"Why are you sabotaging yourself?" She took off to the kitchen.

It was like the Twilight Zone. What the hell was she doing?

She marched straight over and yanked the coffee maker she'd given me out of the wall. Then she stalked back over with it cradled under her arm. I didn't know whether to be pissed or laugh. She was losing it right in front of me.

Cassie's free hand came up and she shoved an index finger in my face. "You don't deserve coffee, asshole!"

She turned to storm out of the apartment. I snagged her lightly by the arm. "Hey?"

"Hey what? Don't touch me." She yanked her arm away but stopped in her tracks.

"I'm sorry. It has to be this way."

She turned around, like she was going through the stages of grief right in front of me. First, she was mad, now she was sad. "No, it doesn't."

"She deserves better. We all know it's true."

"She deserves to be happy. And she was, with *you*."

I looked away. I couldn't look at her. It was easier when she was pissed off. Now, it was just guilt. Guilt I didn't want. I had enough of it in my life already. I didn't know what to say, so I didn't say anything.

"You should at least try. See what happens."

She seemed to have calmed down a little and was maybe thinking a little more rationally.

I sighed and turned. Stared out the window. "I don't want to drag her down. She has dreams and goals. I don't want to keep her from all that."

"You won't. I've seen how she is around you. Well, not really around you. But, I can tell. She's in love with you."

"Don't be ridiculous. We barely know each other."

"*You're* being ridiculous. She's dated plenty of guys and she's never been like this. And I have a feeling you've never felt this way about someone either."

She was right. I knew she was. But, everyone I'd ever gotten close to, I'd hurt. Somehow or some way, I'd managed to fuck it all up.

"Look, do whatever you want." She dumped the coffee maker on my couch. "Keep the damn coffee." She took a few steps through the tiny apartment and stopped in front of the door. "She's going to be at the town Christmas Festival tomorrow. It'll probably be your last chance. In case you were wondering. She accepted a job in Chicago. I didn't tell you any of this."

A wave of ice-cold air hit me in the face when she opened the door and walked through.

I stood there. What was I going to do?

———

I smiled at the computer I had set up in my office space. The door swung open and a UPS guy in his brown shirt wheeled in a dolly with three boxes on it. The first order had just arrived. My smile grew wider.

Truffles.

That's what was in the boxes. Imported from France. I got a sweet deal on them.

I signed off on the delivery and the guy left in a hurry, probably had a truck full of stuff to deliver and not enough hours in the day to do it right before Christmas.

Now, all I had to do was separate them and ship them right back out on their way to individual customers in the U.S. I could sell them for five times what I paid wholesale. The profit was enough to pay the rent for two years.

It was what my life should've been like before I went away. I thought about all the money I could've made the entire time I was away. Years of my life wasted in a cell. All for trying to help someone out. I didn't regret what I did. That lady was safe, even if I had to go to prison and waste away part of my life. That guy couldn't beat on her anymore. I had to look out for myself now, though. I had to guard everything.

Brandon walked in and interrupted me from my thoughts. I got up and started unpacking the boxes.

"This the first order?"

"Yeah."

"You actually look happy. You might even smile."

I didn't look up, just held up a middle finger at him.

He laughed it off. "Things are going well."

"Turning it around. One smelly-ass mushroom at a time." I held up one of the smaller packages.

"How's it going with the girl?"

My eyes shot up to meet his. "Don't, man. Don't ruin the moment."

"What?" He held both hands up in defense. "Was just a question."

"She took a job in Chicago. Better this way."

"Better for who?"

"C'mon."

"You can sit there and pretend to be happy about all this." He stared around the room. "What good is success if you don't have anyone to share it with?"

What was it with all the fucking Dr. Phils in my life?

"Nice one, Mr. Philosopher."

That got another laugh out of him. "It's Christmas time. Maybe you should watch some of those Hallmark movies. Change your mind."

"Jesus." I couldn't even look at him.

He broke out an accent as if he was narrating a film. "The misunderstood bad boy comes to town, down on his luck, fresh out of prison, lands the woman of his dreams and crushes it in the business world. Ditches his leather jacket for a Christmas sweater and a chance at true love against all odds. They fall in love and start making babies…"

I snatched the box cutter off my desk and held it up at him. "I'm gonna fuckin' cut you."

"Easy with the prison talk, Shawshank."

We both died laughing.

"You got the 'shank' part right."

"Do they really do that shit? File down toothbrushes? Make wine in the toilet?"

"You watch too much TV. That's what settling down and getting married gets you."

"So, she took the job?"

I stood up and set the box knife down. "Yeah."

"You could still date."

I glared.

He held his palms up at me once more. "I'm not suggesting you get married, calm down. Just, you could try and see what happens."

I started to say something, and he cut me off again.

"What the fuck are you so afraid of? If it doesn't work out, you just say so. No harm done."

"No harm? Have you ever broken up with someone?"

He stared at me with a blank expression.

"Oh yeah, you married the first vagina that ever let you stick it in."

He snickered yet managed to stay cheery somehow. "Hey, I'm happy."

"I know. It's just, fuck." I unpacked a few more truffles.

"Do what's best for you, man. You deserve to look out for yourself after all the shit you've been through. I get it. But, the right partner by your side—it's a whole new level of awesome. I don't want to see you miss out on something like that. You have enough regrets."

"If I say I'll think about it, will you shut up and help me pack these fucking things up?"

"Definitely."

He walked over, and I grabbed some smaller boxes and started building them. Brandon didn't say anything as we got to work.

I glanced over at him. "Hey?"

"Yeah?"

"Thanks."

"No worries, man."

He was right. Brandon was always right. And he'd stuck by my side when nobody else had. No matter what happened, he was someone I could trust.

LAKE

It was Christmas Eve. My favorite day of the year. A lot of people thought Christmas was the best, but I always loved the day before the most. The anticipation. All the kids running around town, excited about Santa Claus. Families doing things together. The town traditions. That was what it was all about. Christmas Day was always so solitary. Everyone was in their own houses, in their own little bubbles. I loved the community aspect of the holidays. No fighting. No politics. Just people walking around, happy, even when they were rushing to get last minute gifts. They might look annoyed, but there was a feeling, a buzz. Everyone could feel it. Or at least I could.

Maybe I was just an optimist that way, but I loved every minute.

Except for the pit still lodged in my stomach.

Parker.

I couldn't let him ruin Christmas for me. I'd missed out on so much, being so busy all the time. Even when I came home for the holidays I was always studying and didn't get to just relax and breathe it in the way I did when I was a kid.

The festival was tonight. There would be carolers and hot chocolate and Santa would somehow magically show up and see the kids, even though he should be at the North Pole prepping to fly all around the world. The kids didn't question it for a second because it was Santa. He was larger than life.

I'd hang out with Cassie at the festival. She already promised me Parker wouldn't be caught dead there. Not his thing. I wasn't surprised. Maybe it really was just lust and nothing more. How could I be with someone who wouldn't love Christmas, anyway?

I got up and walked through the kitchen.

"Big plans for the day?" Dad walked up and gave me a big hug.

I could tell he was happier when I was home. It was going to break his heart when I left in two days. The design firm I took the job with was out for the holidays, but I wanted to get to Chicago and get things squared away with my apartment. Unpack. All that good stuff. That way I could hit the floor running the day after New Year's.

"Going to hang out with Cassie. Go to the festival tonight. Maybe go see if they need help setting anything up."

"Your mom said the kids are doing some kind of musical thing. They're going to dress up as elves."

I couldn't help but smile just thinking about it. I bet they'd be adorable.

I turned to the Amazon Echo I'd given my parents last Christmas. "Alexa, play Christmas music."

Dad stared at me like I was a crazy person.

It fired up and started playing *White Christmas*.

Dad's eyes bugged out. "That thing has been listening to us for the past year?"

I laughed.

"That's how the robots will take over the world, you know?"

I hugged him, hard. "I love you, Dad."

"Love you too, sweetie."

Cassie burst through the front door right at that moment. No knock. No announcement.

"Hey!"

"Cassie?" Dad held up his coffee mug at her as if to acknowledge her presence.

"Dad." She gave him a nod and a smile, then turned to me. "Ready?"

"Yeah."

"You kids have fun." Dad went back to his newspaper at the table.

I left the Christmas music running for him and grabbed my coat.

———

We stopped for lunch at a little diner in town. It was surreal. I didn't know half the people we saw. Cassie and I used to know every single person when we were kids. We hadn't done much all morning, just walked around town, looking at the decorations.

I never really did that at college. It was just college. You walked to class, to the library, then you drove off campus. Nobody just wandered around town.

I missed that—wandering. I'd miss it again when I moved. I couldn't argue too much. It was the best of both worlds. Chicago was amazing, and I'd have an opportunity to work with big-time clients. I could always drive back home and see everyone and walk around town.

"This is weird, huh?"

Cassie looked up at me. "What?"

"I mean, the town is changing so much."

"It's growing a lot."

"Is it selfish to say I don't want it to? I want it to stay the same as it was."

She looked over the menu. "I guess nothing ever stays the same, really. Even if it does, people change, so it's still different."

A waitress walked over with two cups of coffee without us even ordering them. That's how they did things at the diner. Everyone got coffee.

I looked out and saw some clouds building in the distance.

"Is it supposed to snow?"

"I don't know. Maybe."

"God, it would be perfect."

Cassie took a sip of her coffee. "You don't have to pretend."

"Pretend what?"

"To be so cheery."

"I *am* cheery."

"It's fake cheer." She sat the coffee down. "You're fake cheering me."

I feigned a look of bewilderment. "I am not."

"Lake, you need to get it out of your system, so you can actually enjoy this, and not fake enjoy it. I know you."

I looked away. Maybe I was suppressing certain things, but what else could I do? I couldn't change other people. "What do you want me to say?"

"Say you're sad about Parker and even though you're happy about landing your dream job, you're sad about leaving Hope."

"Well, I *am* sad. About all those things. But, I can't change people. And there's not a huge market for what I love to do here. So, I just have to deal with that. I can't walk around being a Scrooge about it."

"You can't pretend to not care either. Not around me, anyway. I can sense it. You have bad Christmas vibes right now. And I mean that in the nicest way possible."

"Did you just say I have bad Christmas vibes?"

"Yeah, and I'd say it again."

We both laughed.

"God, I know, but what do you want me to do about it?"

"You could always get day drunk. Egg nog is acceptable when the sun is up this time of year."

"I'm not gonna booze it up and then hang out with everyone at the festival later."

"Maybe we could score some weed?"

"You're ridiculous. I probably have a drug test coming up."

Cassie scoffed. "Companies still do those for weed? It's 2018."

I shook my head at her, grinning. She was trying to cheer me up. Or turn my fake cheer to real cheer. It was working a little.

We ordered food and sat there. We didn't do anything but talk about old times and all kinds of stuff for two hours. It was perfect, really. By the time we paid our tab and left I'd almost forgotten about Parker and the fact I had to leave in two days.

It was the best. And that was why Cassie was my best friend.

———

We ended up staying in town until the festival. The sun was just dipping down over the horizon and casting all kinds of oranges and purples all over the sky. Behind us, the sky was still slate gray and I wondered if it was ever going to snow, or just sit back there and tease me.

We walked down the main street, and everyone was bundled up to their necks. The kids all stared around at the lights. It was getting darker by the minute, so we made our way to the small park where the festivities were held. The crowd was way bigger than I remembered as a kid.

The town really was growing fast.

Cassie smiled at me.

"What?"

"You're grinning."

"That's good, right?"

"I think you love Christmas more than anyone I know." Her words turned to white fog in front of her face as the temperature dropped with the sun.

I took in a deep breath of chill air. "Just haven't had this in a while."

"I know."

I looked around. Despite the fact it had clearly grown into a much larger production, it still had the same small-town feel. Mr. Anderson still had his smoker out and sold pork barbecue sandwiches for a dollar. Clearly inflation hadn't tainted the sacred Christmas festival. The same stage they'd used when I was younger was set up for the kids. The same men were unspooling cords and setting up microphones and speakers.

Before long, the Christmas songs were blaring, although they had upgraded to a laptop playing the music instead of a big stereo system. People were beginning to flood in from the side streets and I craned my head around the crowd.

"He'll never show up here. Don't worry."

I turned to Cassie. "Who?"

"Parker."

"I was looking for my parents, but thanks." I nudged her with an elbow to let her know I was messing with her. Fact was, this was exactly what I needed to take my mind off him. Clear my head and make rational decisions.

"Sure you were." She nudged me back just as obvious as I had.

"Bitch," I whispered where nobody else could hear.

"Got that right."

We both grinned at each other, and the kids marched up on the stage.

"Oh my God, they're adorable."

The kids filed up onto the stage. Some of them had Santa beards made out of cotton balls and some of them had elf ears. They all stood in front of the microphones, awaiting instructions from the lady who coordinated everything. A few of them nervously waved to their parents who were all crowded around in front of the stage with cell phones and video cameras.

One boy stuck his tongue out at the crowd and everyone laughed. I wondered if that was the kind of boy Parker was before he became what he was now.

Don't think about him.

The music fired up before I could ignore my own advice and think about Parker some more. It was perfect. The kids all screamed the lyrics to *Jingle Bells* and did their little dance to the song. They all stood frozen, stiff as boards as soon as the song ended while the entire crowd roared their approval.

Between songs, my mom and dad fought their way in next to us.

"Hey, guys!"

Dad kissed me on the forehead. "Merry Christmas, sweetheart. Sorry we're late."

"No prob, it's just getting started."

He turned to Cassie. "Daughter."

"Dad."

They smiled.

Mom gave me a big hug and rubbed her hands on my shoulders to warm me up. It was like I was a kid all over again. We all stood there, watching the children with their pink noses belt out Christmas song after Christmas song.

Dad brought us back hot chocolate, and all I could think to make it more perfect was if it would start snowing.

As the festivities wound down, it was time for the grand finale. I knew the sirens were coming before I even heard them. The red flashing lights danced around the park and off the branches of the trees and everyone's heads turned. The big fire truck headed up the road with Santa Claus on top of it.

Every child's face lit up. Their eyes grew wide and sparkled.

Santa made his way through the crowd shouting "ho ho hos" and waved to everyone.

"Did we get a new Santa?"

"Not that I was aware of," Mom said.

He was in the usual Santa outfit with the huge white wig and beard. Something was different, though. It would make sense that someone would take over. The older Santa was already old when I was a kid, so I figured he had to retire sometime.

I shrugged it off.

Santa made his way to the stage and crouched down to talk to all the kids. He shook their hands and patted them on the head. That was usually the extent of the show, and then everyone would head home and do their own thing. Probably read *Twas the Night Before Christmas*. Tuck the kids into bed. That sort of stuff.

But, something different happened altogether. Something I'd never seen before in all twenty-four of my years.

Santa grabbed the microphone and stared right at me. And past the beard, sitting in the shadow of the Santa hat, were two familiar slate grey eyes.

What the fuck was I doing?

I stood there, frozen stiff for what seemed like an eternity. It hadn't taken much to persuade the old man to let me dress up as Santa Claus. He was a romantic guy, as I imagined most fake Santa Clauses were. Why else would they dress up as Santa?

I told him my predicament. He gave me some long story about how he wooed his own wife some fifty years ago. I had to stuff a goddamn pillow inside the coat to fill the thing out.

Now, here I was.

One shot to make an impression that would last a lifetime.

I couldn't ever remember being so nervous in my life. Butterflies swarmed somewhere in my stomach behind the Santa outfit and giant pillow. I didn't know what to say. I didn't really have a plan. Figured I would wing it.

I'd never been bad at public speaking. Just usually did my thing.

But Lake, standing there, staring back at me. God, she was the most beautiful woman I'd ever seen in my life. I didn't know what to say. "I love you" seemed like the obvious answer, but it was too short. Too abrupt. Something like that needed to be built up to. You couldn't just awkwardly shout it into a microphone in front of an entire town. The first time you say those three words, it has to be like a good story. The "I love you" comes at the climax, after all the suspense and build up, or it's cheapened.

I panicked.

So, I just started singing, full-on acapella. It had to be horrendous.

Christmas Everyday by Smokey Robinson and the Miracles. It was the only Christmas love song I could think of. My mom used to sing it around the house during Christmas season while it played on vinyl in the background.

The crowd parted as I walked toward Lake. She had a hand cupped over her mouth, but I could still make out her auburn-hazel eyes between her gloved hand and the knit beanie she had on over her head. Her brunette hair flowed out the sides in big waves. I focused right on her eyes and everything else faded away.

I didn't give a shit how awful I sounded. Didn't give a damn about anything but her.

When I got about five feet away, big flakes of snow started floating down from the sky. Lake glanced up at the snow, then dropped her hand and smiled. Her eyes darted straight back to mine and tears streamed down her cheeks.

Happy tears.

That's a good thing, right? Fuck it, keep singing.

I got a few feet away. "Baby, I'm in love with you, and if you say you love me too. It would be Christmas every day."

I held the microphone out. All she had to do was say the words and I knew she'd be mine. I could sense it in the air, feel it in her gaze.

Everything slowed down, like time was stopping. The snow floated down through the air in slow motion. The corners of her lips curled up into the most gorgeous smile of all time.

"I love you too." Her voice echoed through the park.

Suddenly, the crowd reappeared around us. I turned and looked at them, smiled, then turned back around. Wrapped my arms around Lake, dipped her back like they do in all the old movies, and kissed her long and hard.

When we released, I stared straight into her eyes, then looked back, held my arm straight out, and dropped the mic right there on the ground, grinning from ear-to-ear. Then I scooped her up, one arm around her knees and one around the upper part of her back, and carried her off toward the street.

———

Halfway to my car, and I could barely walk, but I was determined to carry her the entire way. Part of the problem was our lips were pressed to each other's the entire way. I didn't want to ever stop kissing her. I didn't want to ever stop holding her.

I couldn't remember ever feeling so alive—so happy. It was like a rush of endorphins. We had to look like fools. Santa Claus carrying her through the streets, making out with her the entire time. We didn't care. It was *us*. We belonged together.

I sat her down when we got to the car, then pressed her against the hood and kissed her full on. Not the PG-rated show we gave the crowd. The hands roaming, pillow-getting-in-the-way-of-what-I-needed type kissing. I needed to feel her skin on mine.

Finally, we separated, and I opened the door for her. She climbed in and I waddled my big ass around the car and squeezed into the seat. I needed her in my apartment, in my bed—if we even made it to the bedroom.

I hauled ass out of the parking lot and down the street.

Lake stared at me, still wide-eyed, like she couldn't believe what was happening.

"I love you, too."

That was all she'd said. Those four words.

They were all I needed.

Everything else would work itself out.

I kept my palm on her cheek the entire ride home and alternated between glancing over to her face and the road. She leaned into my hand and closed her eyes.

I whipped into a parking space in front of my complex. "Don't move."

I got out and waddled around once more and opened the door. Scooped her up again. Her arms wrapped around my neck and her cheek nuzzled against mine.

"Is Santa going to do dirty things to me?"

I looked down at her and grinned like the devil. "He came to town." I sat her down in front of my door and pulled her beanie up over one of her ears, then put my mouth next to it. "Now, he's going to come in your pussy."

She exhaled a breathy sigh. "You're still filthy."

I smacked her on the ass and unlocked the door. "You knew what you signed up for."

"Damn right I did."

I opened the door and she shoved me backward through it. I yanked the robe off and let the pillow spill out onto the floor. We were all over each other in an instant. Nothing but a tangle of arms and legs, pushing, pulling —clothes flying everywhere. My cock was already rock hard.

Lake yanked my pants down and went to her knees in front of me in nothing but a white lace bra and panties. She wrapped her slender fingers around my cock and looked up at me with those gorgeous eyes. "Is this my Christmas present?"

I nodded. "It's all yours."

"I think it's the best present I've ever gotten."

My eyes rolled back, and I groaned when she stroked her hand back and forth, then flattened her tongue on my shaft and licked from base to tip. I didn't know how I'd last long enough to get inside her. A few times I had to grab her by the hair and lean down to kiss her, just to give myself a few seconds of reprieve.

Finally, I figured she'd been kind enough and it was time to return the favor. I stripped her bra and panties off her and bent her over the couch. She turned back to look at me and I spanked her on the ass and kneaded it with my fingers. I couldn't help but let out a small groan. God, her ass was perfect. Everything about her was perfect.

"Don't look back here."

I swatted her ass again, just to see my handprint on it.

"Oooh, why not?" She said it like a taunt.

I leaned over her back and got next to her ear. "You don't need to do anything but shut up and come all over my face."

"I like when you're demanding."

"You like when I eat your pussy from behind too. So I guess you get a two-for-one special today. Merry Christmas."

I slid back and went to my knees behind her, then leaned forward and went to work. My tongue flicked and swirled around her clit.

"Oh God, you were right. Merry Christmas to me." Lake's eyes fluttered closed as I worked my tongue faster and faster.

I gripped her inner thighs and spread them apart farther. I could feel her legs starting to tremble, like an electrical current was radiating down to her toes. She was close. I smacked her on the ass again, harder this time.

"Fuck." She breathed the word out on an exhale.

I licked my thumb and swirled it around her clit and leaned to the side, so I could watch every reaction on her face. "You want me to fuck you?"

"God yes."

"You're going to come on my face, then on my fingers, then on my cock, in that order. Got me?"

She nodded furiously.

"Good girl." I spread her thighs apart again and flatted my tongue across her pussy with the tip rested on her clit. I swirled my tongue in lazy circles, building in intensity.

It didn't take long for her hips to start bucking against my face. She tried to shoot forward at the last second, right before her orgasm, as if the intensity was too much to bear, but I gripped her by the waist and yanked her pussy back onto my face. She shuddered and quivered, then thrashed against my grip.

Every muscle in her body tensed up.

"Fuck, Parker."

I would never get tired of her saying my name as she came.

Right as her first orgasm ended, I stood up and slid two fingers inside her. "Now, on my fingers, as promised."

I grabbed a fistful of her hair and wrenched her head back, so I could look down at her eyes, and shoved my fingers in as far as they would go. Her eyes widened then closed at the sudden intrusion. Goddamn, her pussy was so tight. She clenched around my fingers instantaneously. It wouldn't take long for me to finger fuck another orgasm out of her.

I let go of her hair and reached beneath and pinched one of her nipples hard, then hammered my fingers in and out. She started to shake, partially because she had no real control of her body, and partially because I was slamming my palm up against her ass every time I drove my fingers into her.

She bucked back against my hand in time with each thrust. Her pussy was so wet the smacking sounds echoed off the walls. Before long she had her hands splayed out on the couch, clawing for anything she could get hold of.

"That's it, you like fucking my fingers like a little slut?"

"Oh my God. Parker, I'm so close."

I yanked my hand out and smacked her clit a couple times with my palm, then shoved my fingers back in. I curled the tips up to hit her spot just right.

Her legs wobbled, and she jerked forward, like she couldn't take it anymore. I gripped her shoulder and shoved her back into my hand.

"Fuck, Parker." My name lingered on her tongue, almost like a yelp. She could barely even talk. She was panting uncontrollably.

Her pussy walls gripped my fingers so hard I didn't think I'd be able to pull them back out. Her whole body trembled and shuddered. I shoved in harder, as far as I could as I watched the orgasm roll and crest through her entire body, up her spine and down her legs.

Before she could recover, I fisted my cock and lined up behind her. I slapped the head of my rock-hard dick up against her clit. "Now, on my cock."

She was so worked up she couldn't even speak. Her chest fell into the couch, almost like she'd melted into a puddle.

I grabbed her hips and yanked her ass up in the air, then splayed one hand across her back, holding her chest down.

I pushed my clock in slowly, savoring every second of being inside her again. God, I missed her pussy. It was so fucking tight and wet and the euphoria—it was heaven. I looked down and watched as my dick disappeared inside her. I needed more. Needed to be deeper. I wanted as much of her as I could get.

I lifted my foot onto the arm of the couch and shoved in farther.

"Holy shit!" Her face was pressed sideways against the seat cushion.

I bent down and brushed her hair to the side so I could watch her face, then rested my palm against the side of her neck, gently squeezing.

My toes curled against the couch, gripping as hard as I could so I could drive into her harder and faster. One hand on her neck, one gripping her hip, I fucked her as fast and hard as I could. I wasn't going to last long. My balls were already tight and lifted.

The biggest load of my life was already inching up my shaft.

I yanked her up into me as I drove down into her sweet pussy. It was fucking incredible. The best Christmas present of all time. My cock pistoned in and out of her as I fucked her harder and harder. I didn't want it to ever end. I wanted to stay buried in Lake the rest of my life. I wanted to put baby after baby in her and never stop. I wanted to spend the rest of my life with her, making sure every need was fulfilled and that she was taken care of. I wanted her to have anything she wanted.

For the first time in a long time, I was happy. Nothing else mattered, as long as I was with her, living life with her, making a family.

I pulled out to make the moment last longer.

I walked around and sat down on the couch, then leaned back. She looked at me like *why did you stop?*

I pulled her over on top of me, so that she was straddled.

"Do what you want to me."

Her eyes narrowed, and then there was a flicker of recognition. She realized what I was doing.

Every time I'd fucked her, I was always in control. Even when she was in control for a second, I always took over. Always taking what I wanted, as if she was just a disposable lay. Just something to put my dick inside.

Now, she realized I was submitting. I was handing over control, not something that was easy for me to do.

I held my hands up to her, right in front of her face.

She lowered herself down onto me. I groaned. I wanted to thrust up into her, but I didn't. I sat there, motionless, holding my hands up in surrender. Surrendering to her forever. It was a gesture. She knew exactly what it was.

I wanted her, all of her. An equal partnership. Give and take. Something I wasn't good at. I hadn't trusted anyone in a long time, but I did now. I trusted her.

She took both of my wrists in her hands and pushed them back on top of the couch, next to my head.

She rode me, slow and steady, grinding her hips.

I looked her straight in the eyes. "I'm yours."

She crushed her lips into mine. My mouth parted and let her tongue in. She took what she wanted, grinding her hips back and forth while I completely surrendered.

Her mouth worked around to my neck and she licked around my ear.

"What do you want, Lake?"

"You." She breathed in my ear. "All I want is you."

"For Christmas?"

"Forever."

"I'm all yours, then. Forever. Merry Christmas."

She let go of one of my wrists and gripped the back of my hair. Her nails dragged through my scalp. "I know. And I don't want you to be something you're not. Not now. Not ever. So fuck me like I'm your little slut."

I grinned. Fuck, I loved this woman. "Thought you'd never ask." I smacked her ass and drove my cock up into her.

"Fuck, Parker!"

"That's what I'm doing. I'm going to put a baby in you for Christmas."

"Holy shit." Her eyes rolled back in her head.

I wrapped my arms around her and squeezed her tight against my chest, so that she couldn't move. "And there's nothing you can do about it. You're mine." I drove into her rapidly, harder than I'd ever fucked her before.

She tried to speak but it was nothing but garbled gibberish. Her voice vibrated from the impact of my thighs on her ass. At the last second, when I couldn't hold back any longer, I drove up into her and shoved her down on my cock as hard as possible, so that I was as deep as I could get.

I let loose and hot jets of come shot into her tight pussy. She came at the same time and her tight cunt squeezed hard around me. Fuzzy stars danced in my vision. I felt like I was floating on the air. Everything in the world was right.

"Parker. Parker."

All I could hear was my name, over and over on her lips.

I lifted up, keeping my cock buried inside her, then laid her down gently on her back. I pushed her legs up in the air so that her ass was angled toward the ceiling, and I pulled my cock out of her.

Some of my come leaked out the sides of her pussy and I pushed it back in with my fingers, all the while my eyes never left hers.

I held her there so that nothing could escape, then I leaned down and rested my sweaty forehead on hers. "Told you. I'm putting a baby in there for Christmas."

She nodded against my forehead, smiling from ear-to-ear. "You know what we have to do now, right?"

"What's that?"

"Get you one of those ugly Christmas sweaters. Since you're a real-life adult."

"You want another spanking, don't you?"

"Thought you'd never ask."

EPILOGUE

L ake

Christmas Eve, One Year Later

It was hard to believe exactly one year ago was when Parker dressed up as Santa Claus and carried me off from the town festival. So much had changed in our lives. Sometimes, it was still surreal.

I glanced over to see he held our three-month-old daughter, Cassandra. She was named after Cassie, of course. He really had gotten me pregnant. People thought we were insane. The crazy thing was, something had changed in Parker that day. It was like he let go of the past and became a totally different guy, the best version of himself. Well, other than in the bedroom.

I was almost a little worried to give him the news about Cassandra. I thought he might try to keep me from going to work. But, he didn't. In fact, he was adamant about me not giving up on my professional aspirations. I called my boss and we worked out an arrangement. I still had to travel to Chicago quite a bit, but most of my work could be done remotely, outside of meeting with clients. We made it work temporarily.

I was on maternity leave now, but I'd have to go back to work soon.

Parker looked up at me. "Hey, guess what?"

"What?" I couldn't help but smile at the way he seemed to always be guarding our daughter. Like he would protect her from anything in the world.

"I didn't renew my lease today."

My head whipped around to him. "What?"

"Well, I paid for two more months, but after that it's done. I already found a new place in Chicago."

My head spun a thousand different directions. "Wait, what are you saying? We're moving?"

"You're stressed. You don't like traveling and being away. I don't want you to miss moments with Cassandra. You'll never get them back."

"You're moving your business? Can you do that?"

"Of course I can. I'm the boss. There's more money to be made there anyway. I can find bigger clients, work less."

Everything became clearer all at once. All my worries seemed to fade away, all the stress. We'd be together all the time. I ran over to him and gave him a hug so hard I thought I might be smothering him.

"Thank you. God, so much. This makes me so happy. You have no idea."

He cupped my cheek in his palm and stared right into my eyes. "I'll do anything to make you happy. Anything."

We kissed, and then I bent down and dropped a kiss on Cassandra's soft forehead.

My family, together.

It was all I wanted. And it was all coming true, like one of those Hallmark Christmas movies.

———

We pulled up to the festival later that night. One year later. One year after the one that changed my life.

Cassandra was bundled up in more layers than she probably needed. It was Parker's doing. Sometimes I almost felt like a bad parent, the way he seemed to love her. I wasn't sure I'd ever match it. The way he stared at her with adoration twenty-four-seven. I couldn't get too upset, though. He stared at me the exact same way. I knew he'd move heaven and hell for both of us. There was no doubt in my mind.

I stared over at him as we walked toward the crowd. "You're not dressed as Santa this year."

He grinned, like he had ulterior motives. "Nope."

We walked up, and both sets of our parents were there. Parker's friend Brandon was there too with his family, along with Cassie.

Cassie smiled huge when she saw us. "How is Cassie junior tonight?" She snatched her out of Parker's arms. Only she could get away with doing something like that without Parker putting up a fight. He barely let anyone else hold her.

"She's sleepy."

Parker stared at her. "Make sure you keep her head propped up."

"I got it, bro. Back off."

Parker held his hands up in defense. "My bad. Just, she was a little fussy. Make sure she has her pacifier. She might want it."

Cassie shook her head at him. "You gonna let her go to school one day?"

I laughed. "Probably not. I feel bad for the day she brings a date home."

Parker glared at both of us, then walked off, not before giving me a kiss on the forehead. He did smile at both of us at the last second, to let us know he was kidding, then he disappeared in the crowd.

"What is he up to?"

"I don't know." Cassie drew out the last syllable as if she did in fact know.

"God, please don't let him sing again," I said.

"It was pretty horrific."

Brandon's eyes lit up. "He sang?"

Cassie's eyes bugged out at him. "Oh yeah. He sure did."

"I thought it was sweet." I shook my head at them.

Cassie nudged me with her elbow. "You're the only one."

Brandon died laughing. "He always freaked out in music class when we were kids. Hated the way he sounded. Which was a legit fear. Dude has no tone at all."

Cassie glanced over to Brandon. "Where did you guys grow up?"

"Like thirty minutes away."

I was still thinking about Parker singing the year before. It only made the memory better for me. He'd embarrassed himself and didn't care. I couldn't believe he grew up just a half-hour from me my whole life.

The kids filed up on stage, one after another for their performance. It was my favorite part. Parker showed up just then with a tray full of cups of hot chocolate. He passed them out to us.

"What are you up to?" I stared right at him.

He just grinned. "Nothing."

"Yeah, right."

The kids all finished their songs and then it was time for Santa. The bright lights on the firetruck whipped around the trees and the sirens went off. All the kids started to shake with excitement.

The actual Santa made his way up. The old man from when I was a kid. I stared at Parker to make sure he wasn't doing some kind of magic trick or optical illusion.

Santa waddled through the crowd, patting kids on the head, shaking their hands. He took the microphone and looked around at everyone. Then, his gaze fixed right on us.

Oh, what is he doing now?

"Parker, what's happening?"

"No idea." Parker grinned again.

Santa put the mic up to his beard. "I hope everyone has been good this year."

All the kids cheered.

Santa held up a hand to quiet them down. "Well, I can't stay too long. I have a very busy night ahead. But, I have something special I need to do."

He walked right toward us. My heart thumped in my chest.

As Santa neared, huge snow flakes began to float down from the sky. Everyone froze for a moment. There wasn't any snow in the forecast. For a minute, I wondered if Parker managed to make it snow somehow. Did he buy a damn snow machine? There was no way it happened like this two years in a row. It was like an omen.

I looked over at Parker and even his eyes were wide with surprise.

Santa walked up with the mic. "You want to take it from here, son?"

Parker gulped and took the mic.

He stared right at me.

I glanced over, and Cassie had tears streaming down from her eyes while she smiled. Cassandra's grandparents all grinned like they were in on the secret too. I stared at our daughter in Cassie's arms and her eyes were wide open, watching it all take place.

Parker held the mic up. The whole world was a whirlwind, but it was like slow motion all over again. Parker had managed to make time stop once more.

"Lake, I love you. More than anything in the world." He dropped to a knee. "I can't think of a better time to ask you this question than right now."

Heart.

Beating a million-miles-an-hour.

My palms started to tremble.

Parker reached for my hand and handed the mic back to Santa. He pulled the glove off my left hand, slowly, taking his time as if collecting his thoughts.

Then, he reached into his pocket and pulled out a little black box. Santa held the mic up in front of him, wanting to capture everything.

"I will always take care of you and our family. With everything in my heart. I'll keep you safe. I'll provide you with whatever you need monetarily, emotionally, physically." He smiled like the devil when he said the last part.

My cheeks heated a little and I blushed, knowing our parents were standing right there. God, he still managed to maintain that little bit of devilishness in him, and I knew he'd never change completely. And I loved that about him.

"Will you marry me?"

His face went pale, and not from the cold. I stared down at him, the love of my life, asking me to spend the rest of my life with him. It was a no-brainer, but I wanted him to sweat it out a little. I didn't want the moment to ever end.

Finally, I nodded. "Yes."

The whole town went wild. There were whistles and cheers.

Parker opened the box and a gorgeous solitaire diamond winked in the light. He took it out and slid it on my hand. Then, he stood up and took my hand in his. His thumb caressed the ring on my finger.

Brandon yelled, "Kiss her!"

And Parker did.

Did he ever.

The same dip as last year, without the pillow and Santa outfit between us.

When we parted Parker scooped up Cassandra in his arms and pulled her away from Cassie. "She needs her Daddy back." He grinned and gave Cassie a peck on the forehead.

People crowded around and said their congratulations as we fought our way out to the street.

I shook my head at Parker. "You're just full of surprises."

"Oh, like you didn't know it was going to happen."

I really didn't. I just stared back at him.

"You really didn't know? Wow, I can't believe Cassie kept a secret. Or our mothers."

I smiled. "They didn't say a word."

"Well, you're in luck. Because there's more."

"What?" My eyes shot open.

He nodded out toward the street.

I turned my head and gasped. There was a bright white sleigh with bells, along with two huge white horses attached to it.

Parker grinned. "Our ride home."

A man in a black top hat stepped down and helped us up into the sleigh. Then he climbed in and took the reins and we started down the street.

"It's like a Christmas fairytale." I thought my smile might be frozen permanently on my face.

It was perfect. The snow came down in huge white flakes.

Parker turned and caressed my hair, our baby daughter in his other arm cradled up tight with a blanket gently over her face blocking her from the snow.

"Only the best for my queen and my princess."

And we rode off toward our home on Christmas Eve, completely happy, with the whole world ahead of us.

If you'd like more from Alex, grab his boxset and get started with the Cocky Suits Series!

Or you can grab the first book in the Cocky Suits Series, Cocky Playboy.

Cockiest Suits Complete Series
*Includes Devil in a Suit, Playboy in a Suit, Player in a
Suit and Rebel in a Suit

Naughty Girl

Devil in a Suit

Playboy in a Suit

Player in a Suit

Rebel in a Suit

Rock God

Guitar God

A Bad Boy for Christmas

Shagged

Professor's Pet

ABOUT THE AUTHOR

Alex hails from the Midwest and currently resides in
New Orleans.
He enjoys writing steamy romance but more
importantly he enjoys the "research" required to
produce the steamy scenes. If you like filthy-mouthed,
possessive alpha heroes and steamy romance, then he's
the author for you!

Sign up for my newsletter and receive EXCLUSIVE
content throughout the year
subscribepage.com/alex-wolf

Where you can follow me